STAR TREK II®

BIOGRAPHIES

D1384007

William Rotsler

Illustrated with photographs

WANDERER BOOKS
Published by Simon & Schuster
NEW YORK

With gratitude to
BJO TRIMBLE,
without whom this book
would definitely not
have been possible.

STAR TREK® II BIOGRAPHIES
William Rotsler

Photographs courtesy of Paramount Pictures Corporation

Published by WANDERER BOOKS
A Simon & Schuster Division of Gulf & Western Corporation
Simon & Schuster Building
1230 Avenue of the Americas
New York, New York 10020
WANDERER and colophon are trademarks of Simon & Schuster
Designed by Stanley S. Drate
Manufactured in the United States of America

10 9 8 7 6 5 4 3 2 1

Library of Congress Cataloging in Publication Data

Rotsler, William.
  Star trek II biographies.
  Bibliography: p.
  Summary: Biographies of Chekov, Kirk, McCoy, Scott, Spock, Sulu, and Uhura, including exerpts from official records, citations, commendations, letters, historical documents, ship's logs, novels, biographies, autobiographies, news accounts, and other sources.
  [1. Science fiction] I. Star trek II, the wrath of Khan. II. Title. III. Title: Star trek 2 biographies. IV. Title: Star trek two biographies.
PZ7 R753Sp 1982   [Fic]   82-17621
ISBN 0-671-46391-8

Contents

Chekov, Pavel Andrievich

SERIAL NUMBER: SD710-820

PRESENT RANK: Lieutenant Commander
BORN: Moscow, Russia, Terra; 6 March 2145
FATHER: Aleksei Mikhailovich Chekov
MOTHER: Catherine Rykova
SIBLINGS: None
MARITAL STATUS: Unmarried
CHILDREN: None
EDUCATION: Leonid Ilyich Brezhnev Educational Complex,
    Moscow; V.I. Lenin Exceptional School, Volgograd;
    Cosmonaut Preparatory Center, Zvezdnyx, Gorodok;
    Starfleet Academy, Class 103
STARFLEET GRADE AVERAGE: 3.6
PRIMARY LANGUAGE: Russian; also Universal English
COMMENDATIONS:
    Silver Palm with Cluster
    Malenkov Model
    Starfleet Unit Citation, with Cluster
    Starfleet Commendations: 11
AWARDS OF VALOR:
    Procyon Order of St. Mark
    Mother Russian Medal of Distinguished Service
    Entrada Order of San Diego
    Starfleet Star of Conspicuous Gallantry
    Federation Exceptional Service Medal
    United Federation of Planets Golden Sun
COMDEMNATIONS: None
STARFLEET ACADEMY DEMERITS: Three
INTERESTS: Weapons, history, specifically Russian
  history, customs, and accomplishments; vodka;
  Russian Literature
STARFLEET ASSIGNMENTS:
    U.S.S. *Leo Minor*, NCC-614 (Scout), Assistant
      Navigator
    U.S.S. *Shaitan*, NCC-519 (Destroyer), Navigator
    U.S.S. *Enterprise*, NCC-1701 (Heavy Cruiser),
      Navigator

U.S.S. *Nelson*, NCC-1843 (Heavy Cruiser), Chief Navigator

U.S.S. *Reliant*, NCC-1844 (Heavy Cruiser), Chief Navigator

U.S.S. *Enterprise*, NCC-1701 (Heavy Cruiser), Chief Navigator

---

Excerpt from Appraisal Records, Leonid Ilyich Brezhnev Educational Complex, signed by Dr. Anatas Voroshilov Lvov, dated 15 March 2157:

Student Pavel Andrievich Chekov is an impressionable youth, but basically reliable in all situations in which we have observed him, both informal and formal.

We recommend him for higher education to the greater glory of Mother Russia.

Excerpt, diary of Pavel Chekov, dated 29 Dec 2157:

This is the end of my first quarter at V.I. Lenin Exceptional School and I have not done as well as I had hoped. My grade average is 3.9; I was expecting a 4. I must do better in the next quarter.

Today, to celebrate, several of us went to Red Star, the biggest archaeological structure in all Moscow, which means the biggest in Russia, which means the biggest in the world! It houses over a million people!

We went to the top, to the playland there. We were almost a thousand feet above the city, higher than Leningora, much higher than Spirit of Tomorrow or

Kaliningrad. The sky seemed darker there, and you could see stars.

My friend Mischa and I laughed and ate too much and were generally inappropriately jolly.

Excerpt, diary of Pavel Chekov, dated: 17 January 2160:

Irini Galliulin has dropped out of Starfleet Academy. I wonder if I shall ever see her again. I am confused as to her reasons. She said she was dissatisfied with the regimen and discipline, and I know it is not for academic reasons. I'm not certain if I was or am in love with her. It is difficult for me to express feelings of this kind.

Letter, Midshipman Pavel Chekov to Catherine Rykova Chekov, dated 6 October 2161:

My dearest mother:

I know that I have not written you in my regular schedule but (1) the duties of a sergeant-major, even a cadet sgt-maj., are many and often; (2) the final examinations were quite difficult. Many failed. Four did not even try, poor fellows. (3) The terminal was down here in the west end of the barracks, which doubled up the load on the east end; that made it doubly difficult to transmit any letter to you, which is why I am putting this on the Backlog Net, to be transmitted during slack hours, such as the middle of the night. (Though I must say, for the last five weeks there has been *someone* at the terminals even at three in the morning! I know, because I set my alarm to get a try at it.)

I'm getting my first posting tomorrow. I hope it

will be to a cruiser, but of course, it is only to be expected that they want seasoned helmsmen on those most important of vessels. That only makes the eventual assignment all the more desirable.

Starfleet—or so says the rumormongers here—always gives the new midshipmen those dull little scouts, with destroyers being only marginally better. They don't *do* anything important, the big cruisers do that. Oh, they have skirmishes with those fascist Klingons from time to time, but nothing *really* important. I should hate dying for some trivial reason like a violation of the neutral zone. But dead is dead and whether it's glory in a battle to save civilization or falling down on a dock, you will not get any deader.

My love to you, to Father, and to all.

Letter, Aleksei Mikhailovich Chekov to his son, undated:

Greetings to you, my son. My congratulations on your promotion and your transfer to the *Shaitan*. A full helmsman at last! May you always pilot your vessel through safe waters! (Isn't that strange, my son; we have not ceased to make comparisons with surface and atmospheric ships. Perhaps it is because those vessels were more personal. Somehow I cannot see a great starship as a single entity. It is too large to grasp. But perhaps you of the younger generation can.)

Your letter about the encounter with the Preloxin skinworms was most frightening to us here. None of us can imagine such horrors! We see the stories told by returning spacemen on the television. We see the documentaries. We see plays enacted with remarkable effects and we think: It's not real.

Snow is real. Sun is real. Soil is real. But *blue* snow? Different suns? Soil where even the chemistry is strange—can *any* of it be real? We tend to think of it as some fantasy by a writer of fiction, not as something our own son, and friend encounters every day!

We pray for you.

Excerpt, letter from Pavel Chehov to his family, dated 3 Sept 2167:

This is fantastic! I'm only twenty-two and I'm being sent to the *Enterprise!* This is the U.S.S. *Enterprise*, NCC-1701, I am writing about! She's left Deneva and I should contact her en route, at Starbase 5. The rumormongers say that the captain, James Kirk, lost a brother on Deneva and is transporting his nephew Peter to Starbase 5 to be transhipped to Earth. Then we'll be on our way toward Altair VI, then out toward Halka.

The *Enterprise* is partway through a five-year mission, so I should return within a shorter time. The responsibility will be enormous, but not beyond my capabilities. I will remember you all, and love you, at all times.

I must punch this into the squirt-transmitter computer right away and I heard over the loudspeaker that *Rothstein* has docked and she is my "bus" to Starbase 5. Tell Inga I could not find the words to write, but if she has any sense she will find some nice sensible bureaucrat and settle down somewhere along the Black Sea.

Excerpt, The Voyages of the U.S.S. Enterprise, by John Griffin:

Pavel Chekov was the brightest of the young midshipmen in that year's class at the Academy. He was very proud of being Russian, even to the point of forgetting that Russians did not accomplish or invent everything.

He was always enthusiastic, but kept his enthusiasm suppressed to conform to his accepted idea of the decorum expected from a Starfleet officer.

He served aboard the *Leo Miner*, a scout ship, then the destroyer *Shaitan*, before accepting assignment to the *Enterprise*, already en route on her five-year mission of exploration and discovery.

Letter, Pavel Chekov to his family, undated but probably circa 2167-8:

Dear loving family:

Starfleet has sent your accummulated letters along via subspace squirt, piggybacking on the sine curve of official signals. Pretty nice, huh? A Russian must have thought of that economy.

First, to answer your questions, then to what I am doing.

I am alive and well, although I sometimes have a difficult time believing I am here, aboard this fantastic ship, or in some kind of dream. Tell Anton yes, there are women aboard, but we are so much busy that our social life is not all we younger officers would like.

I am bunking with Lieutenant Sulu, Hikaru Sulu. He's a Hawaiian-Japanese, an American, though he can be most charming and a good companion at times. He rarely drinks, however. I offered our chief engineer, Mr. Scott, some of my vodka, but he called it something insulting—in a jolly way, however— and prefers his own foul Scotch.

Sulu and I have been practicing karate, both standard and null-space. He still manages to best me at null-space handball, but I am closing the gap. Doing well, in fact, considering he has been practicing much longer.

As to Greta's question about sports and games, see above, but also tell her we have the latest computer simulators—at least the newest as of leaving orbit at Earth—*plus* we have some secret compugames thought up by the tactical and strategy services division. It only takes a bit of imagination and time to reprogram them into real games!

Olga wanted to know about the captain. Well, he is very good. From what you say, the stories of his voyage are only now being released by Starfleet Command, but I assure you, you will be hearing more of Captain James T. Kirk and his crew aboard the *Enterprise*.

As to what I have been doing, mark this. (And you need not suspend your disbelief, either, Olga.)

You've already read about our trip to Vulcan, and that most astonishing encounter with the god Apollo. We then encountered a very strange object, capable of extended spaceflight. It called itself the *Nomad*. It had destroyed several planets and was heading roughly toward our Solar System when we met it.

A battle ensued, and I am not bragging when I say

it was very active and deadly. However, when Captain Kirk identified himself in an attempt to stay the destruction, the *Nomad* broke off its attack . . . thinking that the captain was its creator!

We brought this device aboard—it was astonishingly small, not much larger than Ivan—and so powerful! It wiped out Lt. Uhura's memory, killed our Chief Engineer, then "repaired" him back to life, and did a great deal of mischief and destruction.

Mr. Spock employed the Vulcan mind touch and learned something most astonishing: that the *Nomad* was an early twenty-first-century probe developed by a Jackson Roykirk. It has been programmed to seek out new life and report back. (Of course, this was before the warp drive.)

Nomad had been damaged by a meteor and just drifted until it met an alien probe from a race we are unable to identify. This was *Tan Ru*, a soil sterilizer. The two machines combined, using their self-repair capabilities to create an unique machine, a "changling," as Spock called it.

Nomad's memory banks had been damaged, and somehow the probe thought it still had to seek out life, but also to destroy anything not perfect. Our Captain Kirk took a dangerous chance in pointing out that he was not "the Kirk," the Jackson Roykirk *Nomad* had thought he was, and therefore the probe was not perfect either. Since the machine made the mistake, it was therefore not perfect itself and, confused by Captain Kirk's logic, it blew itself up.

Then we got involved with something so complex I do not think my writing skills are capable of explaining in the few words given me on these signal messages. But it concerned alternate universes and is much too classified to tell more.

We found a paradise on Gamma Trianguli VI that proved not to be one, in a most explosive manner, and then a doomsday machine that was breaking up planets for fuel. On Pyris VII we found some deadly illusionists. We met Harry Mudd and his band of beautiful androids—Captain Kirk had met him before and thought him safely in prison.

Then we met Zefrem Cochrane! Yes, *the* Zefrem Cochrane, still alive and living on a planet that I assume Starfleet would just as soon keep quiet about. We undertook the difficult task of taking a lot of ambassadors to the Babel Conference, where some decisions of vital importance to the Federation were to be made. But the course of true diplomacy does not run smooth. I did get to meet Mr. Spock's parents. Did you know he was the son of *Ambassador* Sarek and a Terran woman? Seems that Sarek had not spoken to Mr. Spock for eighteen years, but it all worked out and we were successful.

We're on to Capella IV, which will give us a kind of vacation, as it is only to negotiate a mining treaty. But we hear the people there are extremely warlike—but with a far lower technology than Starfleet, so don't worry—and are extremely tradition-bound. Being Russian, I can understand that. There are times when I say to myself, "What am I doing here? I should be at home, advancing Russia toward the twenty-fourth century." But then, I look at the forward screen and I see that great, fantastic rush of stars toward us and I *know* why I am here!

My love to you all. Please continue to write, though I know the time between letters is long.

Excerpt, Burnt by a Hundred Suns: The Story of Pavel Chekov, by Beverly Beachwood:

When Marco Polo traveled to China, it was as strange as the *Bonaventure* going to Alpha Centauri. He went with his father and uncle, but only historians remembered. When Magellan sailed around the Horn, when Drake and Cook clefted the waters of the Pacific with her fragile wooden boats, people remember only the name and history of the captains. Who were the other captains of the *Pinta* and the *Santa Maria?* Who were the men with Amundsen, with Balboa, with Erikson and Vasco da Gama and Scott?

But came the dawn of the age of the media and we know intimately those who lifted first from Earth, know their names and faces and histories: Shepard, Gargarin, Glenn, Armstrong, Aldrin, Collins. We know and have records on every man and woman aboard the *Bonaventure*, complete with videotape interviews, holographs, and biographies.

Thus we know a very great amount about the officers and crew of the U.S.S. *Enterprise*, that extraordinary ship of the line that has figured so prominently in the history of space exploration of the United Federation of Planets. The *Excalibur* fought more battles with the Klingons, the *K'Hotan* practically single-handedly stopped with Romulan advance. The *Saratoga* discovered the Koris and straightened out the Tellar-Throbian war. The *Nelson* defended the Federation in five different engagements. The *Endeavor* brought new distinction to Starfleet with its handling of the Quinn crisis. But it has been the *Enterprise* that has captured the imagination and interest of our people. Its exploits, successes, and adventures have been chronicled and lauded and discussed throughout the Federation. This is the most glorious of all ages—the Age of the Starship, when literally the universe is unfolding before us. And the U.S.S. *Enterprise* has been at the heart of that exploration and expansion.

But why a biography of one who is, after all, a minor character in the cast of this great adventure into the final frontier? Because he is *not* a minor character. The inscrutable Spock, the glamorous Uhura, the steadfast Scott, the irascible McCoy, the athletic Sulu, and that finest of captains, James Kirk, have all been fine-toothed by dozens of writers, reporters, and official chroniclers.

But it is Chekov who—excepting Spock—is the most unusual of the main officers. He comes from a culture much different than the others. Even Noyota Uhura's background is closer to, say, Kirk's, than is the Russian Chekov's.

History is an accretion of fact and fable. That the survivors write history has long been a demonstrable fact. But in this age of Instant Reporting, Immediate Gratification, On-the-Spot Analysis, Hyperbole, and Media Glut, there is still a need to find the True Facts.

Memory is the way we file the past, and you know how well most people file. But if you gather in enough facts, interview enough eyewitnesses, make enough correct deductions, you arrive, at last, at an approximation of the truth.

That is what we have done here, as best we could.

Excerpt, letter from Pavel Chekov to Catherine Rykova Chekov; dated 23 May 2169:

I am saddened by the completion of our voyage. It seemed too short, too abrupt. The *Enterprise* went into drydock for repair and retrofitting and I had a joyous month with you, my family. Now I am posted aboard the *Nelson* (NCC-1843) a new and excellent ship under Captain Susan Haseltein, who was in the same Starfleet Academy class with Captain Decker.

I miss the *Enterprise*. I suppose it shall never quite be the same again. I felt that way about my Academy class. We were special, we faced adversity together. (Did I mention that I found Irini Galliulin? She was with a group who were seeking a mythical planet called Eden, but their leader, Sevrin, was a carrier for sythococcus novae, a virulent bacillus strain—no, don't worry, Dr. McCoy says I'm fine! Eventually, Mr. Spock, as resourceful as ever, actually found a planet called Eden! Unfortunately this was not a real "Eden," as the plant life was coated with a natural acid extruda. Some of Irini's group were killed. Sevrin committed suicide but the rest were beamed back, immunized, and transported to Edward Northridge's colony, newly opened to immigrants, and Irini is, I presume, happily homesteading in a *kind* of Eden.)

So I'm on the *Nelson*. It's good, but I still miss the *Enterprise!*

Letter, Anton Sergeyevich Rykov to Pavel Chekov, dated 1 Oct 2172:

It is with great regret that I inform you that your father, Aleksei Mikhailovich Chehov, died during a accident in the Moscow-Kamchatka traffic corridor. A Zvezdá Syémdesat had a navigation computer malfunction and dropped two lanes, striking our father's Vózdukh-pyát, killing all three hundred and forty-two aboard.

He was buried in the family plot Sunday, with many in attendance. Your mother has not yet cried, but did express a desire to see you. It is at times like these that we most regret your selfish desire to roam the spaceways in an irresponsible manner.

We will expect sufficient notification of your arrival to prepare, should you choose to respond to this message.

Subspace message from Lt. Commander Pavel Chekov, aboard the U.S.S. Reliant, to Anton Sergeyevich Rykov, Moscow, Russia; dated 5 Oct 2172:

My dear Uncle Anton:

I have sent a separate message of condolence to Mother, and I do thank you for your signal regarding Father. However, I must protest your accusation that I am selfish and irresponsible in my career in Starfleet.

If no one ever wanted to go see what was on the other side of the mountain, if no one wondered if they could make things better, if no one sought to change things, we would all still be peasants under the heel of the Tzar!

We are no longer the people who bent our backs to the whip of Cossacks. We are a free people, freer than any in the history of the world! We can not only change our lives, but change the lives of whole peoples, entire planets, systems of planets, the very fabric of the universe!

We have *choice!* While our forefathers were the sons of peasants, the grandsons of peasants, the great-grandsons of peasants, and so on back, *we* are different! You did not follow in the traditional footsteps of your family.

But I do not condemn you for changing from the traditional career of the Chekov line—why do you condemn me? Are you jealous? Do you feel left out of the flow of things? I cannot help that. You are in many ways my superior. You could have chosen your path, as did I. The greatness of the Russian people today is in acknowledging and assisting in the development of the capabilities of its brighter children, and you were certainly that.

Are you jealous of the popularity of the *Enterprise,* in the matter of V'ger if no other? Are you envious of the media coverage of me on my shore leave? I cannot help that, either. I was part of a team, not a star player. If there is glory it is to Mr. Spock and Captain Kirk, and to Captain Decker.

Because you are there you feel responsibility for Mother and, knowing you, now the entire family that remains on Earth. But we each must lead our lives. My choice has been space, yours has been what it is. Both may be right, both may be wrong. It is only in your heart do you find an answer.

I am aboard the *Reliant* now (NCC-1844) with

Captain Terrell, from the United States of Africa, commanding. The assistant communications officer is Marta Usubekov, from the Transcaucasian Republic. If you know anyone from there you might pass the word that she is considering marriage with me. If so, we will apply for Marital Status Flight Arrangements. Tell our mother, please, that Marta shares our family's faith and beliefs.

We are en route to Ceti Alpha VI for routine survey, and I shall write again soon.

Excerpt, Official Debriefing of Lieutenant Commandar Pavel Chehov, by Commodore Ridley Normand, dated 1917–2183 (Declassified: 29–7–2183):

RN: You were a serving officer on U.S.S. *Reliant* at the time of this incident?

PC: Yes, sir.

RN: Explain in your own words.

PC: Yes, sir. We arrived at Ceti Alpha VI, and I beamed down with Captain Terrell. It was a desert planet, barren and harsh, with strong winds. We discovered a makeshift shelter, which surprised us. We entered and found it empty. We saw rather battered life-support equipment, stored food, and . . . and then I made a discovery which shocked me.

RN: Go on, Commander.

PC: I discovered a piece of equipment marked *Botany Bay*.

RN: The sleeper ship?

PC: Yes, sir, the one which pre-Federation forces had used to send Khan Noonian Singh into exile after his overthrow. He had once, from 1992 to 1996, been the absolute master of a quarter of the Earth, from South Asia to the Middle East. He was one of the supermen bred selectively by scientists during the Eugenic Wars. They . . . they sent him off in a sleeper ship with some of his more fanatic followers, also genetic supermen and women. That was over two hundred years ago.

RN: I read the account of the *Enterprise*'s meeting with the *Botany Bay*—a most aptly named vessel. Your Captain Kirk barely managed to defeat him and exile him to Ceti Alpha V.

PC: Yes, sir. But then, as we tried to leave in a hurry, they returned. They were dressed in patched clothes, made from bits of upholstery, drapes, other materials, and ornamented with fragments of circuitry, wiring, and spaceship parts.

RN: Go on. You were captured?

PC: Yes, sir. They were incredibly strong and moved with surprising swiftness. They took us inside, and Khan revealed himself. I was doubly shocked, for he recognized me! I have no explanation for that, as I came aboard the *Enterprise* after the contact with the *Botany Bay*. I recognized him from ship's records and from historical photographs. But he *is* a kind of superman and . . . he might have memorized the faces of the entire Starfleet.

RN: I doubt that, Commander, but go on.

PC: We then learned that Ceti Alpha IV had exploded—no explanation given, perhaps a strike by a very large asteroid—and the effect was to shove Ceti Alpha V into roughly the orbit of the sixth planet, and it farther out. It devastated the surface of what had been quite a pleasant world. They had only had six months there, Khan said. His wife—she had been

Lieutenant Marla McGivers, Ship's Historian on the *Enterprise*—

RN: Yes, I am aware of that. It is really somewhat of a scandal, a Federation officer . . . Never mind. Please continue.

PC: The next part is, is quite painful to remember, what little of it I do remember. Khan placed the larva of the Ceti eel in our helmets and clamped them around our heads. It, it crawled in my ear . . . and into my, my brain . . .

RN: Stay calm, Commander.

PC: I, I don't remember much after that, just . . . just flickerings. Both Captain Terrell and I were in Khan's control. The larva buries itself into the brain and . . .

RN: Commander.

PC: One becomes susceptible to exterior control, Commodore. I was not responsible for my condition. I know that I appeared reasonably calm. I was told that by Dr. Carol Marcus and by Captain Kirk.

RN: Using you and Captain Terrell, Khan gained control of the *Reliant*. The crew was killed as soon as Khan's supermen and women learned how to pilot the ship.

PC: Yes, sir. They learn amazingly fast.

RN: Khan held a deep hatred for James Kirk, I understand. No doubt as a result of his defeat fifteen years earlier by someone whom he considered inferior.

PC: Yes, sir, so I understand. Khan learned about the Genesis Project and knew that he had the ultimate weapon.

RN: Yes, that is classified Ultra-Purple, Commander.

PC: Yes, sir. As I said, I do not remember much until the Ceti eel larva was removed by Dr. McCoy and I . . . well, I was in something of a daze for a time. We had transported down into an articial cavern beneath the surface of a lifeless moon, where Dr. Marcus and her staff of Space Lab Regula One had been conducting experiments. Khan stole the Genesis machine and left us to die, or so he believed.

RN: But Dr. Marcus had progressed further than Khan had realized, hadn't she?

PC: Yes, sir. They had created a underground world of sorts. Really quite beautiful. Dr. Marcus called it the Genesis Cave, but Captain Kirk later jokingly called it "Pellucidar."

RN: Ah; from the Burroughs stories. Go on.

PC: It's a little vague, sir, I was unconscious much of the time and some of it . . . Well, they told me afterwards.

RN: That's all right, Commander, we are interrogating everyone concerned.

PC: Very well, sir. Captain Kirk had tricked Khan. The *Enterprise* had been hidden precisely on the opposite side of the planet from the *Reliant*. We beamed aboard, and the fight began. I was feeling better and eventually felt good enough to join the bridge crew. A personal observation, sir?

RN: Go on.

PC: I felt that Captain Kirk was grateful for my return. I know that sounds egotistical, but . . . well, most of us had gone through a lot together in the old days. We knew each other, knew our strengths and, yes, our flaws. I think he was glad to get "the old crew" together again.

RN: Every commander likes a reliable command. You headed for a nebula?

PC: Yes, sir. We were at a disadvantage. The electronic confusion of those highly charged gas particles made it a kind of fog. It was very much like two submarines, back in the twentieth or twenty-first century, fighting each other blindly in water, with only the most primitive of sensors and weapons.

RN: Go on.

PC: There was a personal tragedy to a friend of mine during that battle. Mr. Scott's nephew, a midshipman on his very first voyage, was killed. Khan's phaser attack was devastating to us. We were pretty well shot up, caught with our screens down early on. But Mr. Spock and the Captain devised a plan during Khan's negotiations, when he thought he had us where he wanted us. He wanted to trade Kirk for our lives, but the Captain tricked him, used the Starfleet secret screening shutdown code to drop the *Reliant*'s screens and cripple her.

RN: Khan was killed?

PC: He killed himself, sir. He used the Genesis device. We had four minutes to get away and our warp engines had been disabled. That's when Mr. Spock . . . when he . . .

RN: Take it easy, Commander.

PC: He was the bravest of men, sir. He knew what he was doing. It was not like some who are called heroes, who do things because they are unaware of the danger, or are angry. No, he knew he was killing himself. He sacrificed himself to save us, Commodore. Coldly and . . . logically . . . he weighed one against the many and he, he did what he had to do.

Courage is knowing the dangers and doing it any-way.

RN: Indeed, Captain Spock acted above and be-yond the call of duty. But, Mr. Chekov, there is one thing you neglected to mention.

PC: Sir?

RN: While in the Genesis cave did not Captain Terrell attempt to kill Captain Kirk?

PC: Sir, I don't remember that clearly. But Captain Terrell was no more responsible for that than for anything else. When those larva are . . . you . . . It's horrible, sir. You are helpless. You are an automa-ton. It is to Captain Terrell's eternal credit that he used every ounce of his willpower to resist Khan's order, then, when he knew he was weakening, that Khan would win, that he would be forced to kill Captain Kirk, he, then he killed himself, sir. He too, sir, is a man of great courage.

RN: Why did you not say this sooner?

PC: It's hazy in my memory, sir. But . . . but that's not the real reason. Things become distorted. Per-haps all anyone would remember is that one star-ship captain attempted to kill another. I . . . I thought it best to . . .

RN: Commander, allow me to remind you that it is Starfleet Command who will decide what shall be part of the record and what shall not. As it is, Captain Terrell will receive appropriate commenda-tions and awards.

PC: Yes, sir.

RN: You are continuing to serve aboard the *Enter-prise?*

PC: Yes, sir!

Kirk, James Tiberius

SERIAL NUMBER: SC937-017CEC

PRESENT RANK: Admiral
BORN: Farside Base, Luna, 28 July 2132
FATHER: Eugene Claudius Kirk
MOTHER: Marjorie Wimpole
SIBLINGS:
> George Samuel Kirk
> (James Tiberius Kirk)
> Michele Suzanne Kirk

MARITAL STATUS: Unmarried
CHILDREN: David James Marcus (m: Carol Marcus)
EDUCATION: Thomas Jefferson Elementary School, Farside Base, Luna; Junipero Serra Elementary School, Santa Barbara, California, Terra; Oxnard Union High School, Oxnard, California, Terra; University of Southern California, Los Angeles, California, Terra; Starfleet Academy, Class 92
STARFLEET ACADEMY GRADE AVERAGE: 3.8
PRIMARY LANGUAGE: English; also Universal English, French, German
COMMENDATIONS:
> Palm Leaf of Axanar Peace Mission
> Grankite Order of Tactics, Class of Excellence
> Prantares Ribbon of Commendation, First and Second Class
> Designated Hero, Empire of Thrace
> Silver Palm with Cluster
> Plixar, Hydrogen Class
> Martian Colonies Award of Merit
> Starfleet Unit Citation, with Three Clusters
> Starfleet Commendations: 84

AWARDS OF VALOR:
> Karagite Order of Heroism
> Procyon Order of St. Mark
> Ananar Medal with Nova
> Starfleet Citation of Conspicuous Gallantry, 1st Class

Federation Exceptional Service Medal
United Federation of Planets Golden Sun
United Federation of Planets Medal of Honor
United Federation of Planets Golden Medal of Honor

CONDEMNATIONS: Three

STARFLEET ACADEMY DEMERITS: Nine

INTERESTS: Artifacts of ancient worlds, specifically
Earth; null-gravity handball; history, specifically
Terran

STARFLEET ASSIGNMENTS:

U.S.S. *Farragut*, NCC-1702 (Heavy Cruiser), Assistant
Engineering Officer

U.S.S. *Republic*, NCC-1371 (Heavy Cruiser), Assistant
Science Officer

U.S.S. *El Dorado*, NCC-1722 (Heavy Cruiser), First
Officer

U.S.S. *Saladin*, NCC-500 (Destroyer), Commanding
Officer

U.S.S. *Enterprise*, NCC-1701 (Heavy Cruiser),
Commanding Officer

Starfleet Academy, staff

U.S.S. *Enterprise*, NCC-1701 (Heavy Cruiser),
Commanding Officer

Starfleet Academy, faculty

U.S.S. *Enterprise*, NCC-1701 (Heavy Cruiser),
Commanding Officer

**Excerpt, Where No Man Has Gone Before; The
Autobiography of James T. Kirk:**

I was not unusual. Like others around me I
wanted to go into space. Twelve centuries before I
would have set forth in a Viking boat. Six hundred

years ago I would have headed west, toward the edge of the world. Four hundred years ago I would have been one of those who set out across the sea of grass, down from the Cumberland Gap, setting a metaphoric sail for the golden land of California. Three hundred years ago I would have tried to be an astronaut. Two hundred years ago I would have attempted to sail in a sleeper ship to the far stars.

But I was lucky. I was born into the age of the spacewarp, to starships and the men and women to run them. I was only unusual in one thing from those around me: I *really* wanted to go.

There are men who dream of writing great novels and women who dream of great songs. There are those who try and those who fail. But you do not fail if you try, only if you do not try. I tried.

Excerpt, (Declassified) Service Record Evaluation by Dr. Leopold Sachs, dated 30 June 2159:

. . . A most exceptional officer by every standard of Starfleet. His feeling of responsibility toward his ship and his crew is remarkable in its intensity. In one sense this is his Achilles' heel, yet it is mainly his strength.

. . . Subject has a tendency to fall in love easily, despite his exterior facade of tough leadership, tight control, and personal standards of conduct. His oft-demonstrated susceptibility reveals, perhaps more than any other factor, subject's romanticism. (See "What Lies Beyond: The Factors of Love in the Motivation of Intraspace Selection Methods," in *The New England Journal of Medicine Annual Review*.) To capsulize: To leave the known and safe requires a certain kind of mind set combined with sufficient motivation. Not everyone can leave what they know and willingly sail toward the total unknown. While some are forced into it, they hate it. It has been the policy of Starfleet Command to seek out those who are a combination of the seeker, the romantic, and the pragmatic survivalist.

Excerpt, transcription of interview with Marjorie Wimpole Kirk, mother of James Kirk, by NBC-TV, dated 11 Dec 2174:

NBC: Why do you think your son wanted to go to the stars?

MWK: Well, he was born on Farside, where the light from Earth cannot be seen. The stars there . . . well, they are magnificent. Astonishing. Intimidating to some. He grew up looking at them day and night, out every port. Earth was something he saw on a television screen or in a hologram.

NBC: You mean, Earth was an abstraction?

MWK: Yes and no. He grew to love it when we went downside. But it was always rather an exotic place to him, not Good Old Earth as we knew it. I suppose that gave him a taste for . . . exotic places, strange people, unusual life forms. I remember the first time he saw a skunk. For some reason he'd never seen or paid any attention to pictures of them—

NBC: And you have none on the Moon Colonies.

MWK: That's right. He saw that thing and—you guessed it—it was his first encounter with a hostile life form!

NBC: Did you encourage him in any way to go into space?

MWK: No, he didn't need it. It was something we all understood. If anything, I guess we discouraged him. Didn't work, I'm happy to say. His brother George was the same, only he set himself limits. George wanted to go out, see some of what there was to see, find a fine woman and settle down on some interesting planet and have a family. So you see, not every person who longs to travel to the stars wants to keep *on* traveling to the stars.

NBC: George and his wife, Aurelan Swift, are dead now?

MWK: Yes, but their son, Peter, he's about to enter the Starfleet Academy soon.

NBC: How did your son James get into the Academy? He was rather young, wasn' he?

MWK: Yes, quite young. Of course, Starfleet has its share of youthful geniuses—geniuses in math, in computers, in science. I'm not saying Jimmy was a genius, but he certainly wasn't dumb. I suppose . . . um . . . well, if you were to look for a single label I'd say, um . . . generalist. He specialized in everything. Of course, history always fascinated him. "Those who do not know history are condemned to repeat it," that was one of his favorite sayings.

NBC: So he entered the Academy . . . ?

MWK: Yes. He was thought quite exceptional. Jay Mallory was a young Admiral then—about Jimmy's age now, I'd say. He was the one who really sponsored Jim.

NBC: Wasn't there a slight, ah, scandal involving him while he was at the Academy?

MWK: Oh, dear. Things are never really forgotten, are they? Which one do you mean?

NBC: There are more than one?

MWK: (Laughter) Oh, yes, I'm afraid so. He was always, um, popular with women. His father was a little like that. But I suppose, well, I suppose you mean the computer simulator scandal.

NBC: Yes.

MWK: Well, it *wasn't* a scandal, you see. He reprogrammed the computer so that he *could* win, that's all. Not what the staff had in mind, but he did get a recommendation for ingenuity.

NBC: Now, about the women . . .

MWK: Oh, no! Jim knew a lot of women. He attracted them, and when he was a cadet and midshipman, too, not just when he got to be a captain. But he wasn't serious about any of them.

NBC: He has stated, in his autobiography and elsewhere, that he was in love with several women.

MWK: Yes, that's true . . . but not enough to settle down. I doubt if Jim will *ever* settle down until they drag him off a bridge. And you know what? These warp-drive ships are getting less expensive all the time. I wouldn't be at all surprised if he just kept on doing what he's been doing, but as a civilian.

NBC: What do you mean?

MWK: Get himself a nice speedy little ship, maybe one of these Explorer-class ships, or perhaps recondition an old scout ship, something like that. Then just take off again. There are plenty who would go with him, I'm certain.

NBC: Whom do you mean? Women?

MWK: I wouldn't know about that, but I meant his

shipmates. People he knew, people he trusted. Jim's always been a great one for trusting people. But not in any foolish way. "People are people, he said to me once. You learn what they are like, then trust them to behave like themselves". Then he laughed and said, "Except when they surprise you." But I wouldn't be the least surprised if he just up and took off. Probably call the ship the *Enterprise II*. He really loved that starship.

NBC: Tell us more about him at the Academy.

MWK: Well, he worked hard. Played hard, too. He was very ambitious, but it was, at least to me, a curious yet commendable ambition. If he got somewhere, into some position of command, he would have more control over his life. A starship captain is one of the last free creatures, yet . . . yet in many ways the most bound of entities. He commands immense power—a starship like the *Enterprise* can devastate a planet. Yet he must use that power most selectively.

I think Jim is the perfect starship commander. He is strong; men and women follow him, not because of his rank, but because they want to, because they see in him a true leader. Look at his long friendship with Mr. Spock. Jim certainly acknowledged the Vulcan's superior intellect, but the two of them were a *team*, each complementing the other. Spock saw in Jim that quality of leadership which the whole System, the whole Federation has admired.

NBC: You sound the proud mother.

MWK: Of *course*, I am, Mr. Warren! Wouldn't you be the proud parent of such a man? We bore a famous son, but a *good* man, too, a kind and sensitive man. He did what he had to do.

Excerpt, letter from Lieutenant José Domingues to Lieutenant James Kirk; dated 3 July 2151:

Hola!

Heard you were aboard the *Farragut!* Garrovick is a tough captain—aren't they all?—but fair enough, I guess. I'm on the *Mars* (NCC-525, Destroyer, in case you want to answer) and doing well.

Saw Janice Lester my last time in Lunaport, and José Tyler, too. Oh, and Admiral Byron Komack is now head of Starfleet Academy. Heard Cat Spaulding got married—some *civilian*, would you believe, with his own ore lugger working out of the Asteroid Belt. Saw the old *Bonaventure* while we were in Alpha Centauri orbit. What a great old ship!

Well, *vaya con Dios, amigo!* I'll see you when I see you.

Excerpt, Kirk, by José Domingues:

We finally got together when the *Republic* limped into repair orbit at Tellar. They'd been nipped by a Klingon dreadnought, a real zipper of the *Kl'ar* class. Result of a little dispute over *exact* boundary of the neutral zone. I don't think the Klingons were correct, but how do you get it straight after the shooting is over? The winners usually write the history and there were no winners in this mess.

The *Republic*'s bottom screens were damaged, giving them some hull damage, but, according to my ol' buddy Kirk, the Klingon ship lost its artificial gravity and they went off into subspace holding on to the ceiling.

We did a bit of drinking that time. Percy Stone

was the captain, and he just left aboard a skeleton crew to keep the repair monkeys out of things and beamed everyone down to Tellar.

Tellar in those days had a liberty port that was maybe the best in the "civilized" Federation. (There are some others out near the edges that are pretty wild!) Telmachus is the port, and they had everything then: bars, dance halls, heavy-gravity chambers, computer-simulators the like of which we'd never seen, combrotanks, Orget synthesizors, blit races, go-down ships, Freelers, Tellarian shiver bands, Coridan shimmer stars, infinity chambers, illegal ghlots, everything—and I mean *everything*.

We started at one end and darned near made it to the other! Somewhere we acquired a blit racer and three women, one of them a Freeler. We sang "Federation Forever" and "Modern Major-General" and the Freeler fight song.

We lost the blit racer, acquired a nav officer off the *Cortez*, then lost her somewhere. The Freeler got into a fight with a ghlot smuggler and we wrecked some bar that, if memory serves, was called The Slanshack. We ended up—and I confess here to a certain loss of memory over transitions—with two young women, one from Fond du Lac, Wisconsin, and the other from Bombay, India, who were expert blit racers. So there we were, riding behind our "dates" on blits, going far, far too fast on the Moebius strips, crossing and criss-crossing, coming *this* far from boppo time.

The rest is a merciful blur of this and that. But I must say one thing: Jim Kirk is a man to have at your back in a Tellarian bar when an eight-foot

Bellsarian decides he wants your head and a three-foot Transor with a prosthetic arm wants to chug you into Corp food.

Excerpt, Starship Crewmen Under Stress, by Dr. David Marano:

. . . Aboard the *El Dorado* at that time was a young officer who was to later become slightly conspicuous: James Tiberius Kirk. He was First Officer then, serious on the job and studiously unserious off the job.

The *El Dorado* (NCC-1722) was a Heavy Cruiser of the MK-IXA subclass. Prince Fiawol, Subarch of Trexlor, was commanding, a most impressive and experienced officer. An Andorian, he commanded an experimental ship in that the crew was of mixed racial stock: a *Homo sapien* (Kirk) was First Officer; a Tellarian was Science Officer; a Rigellian was Medical Officer; another Rigellian was Navigation Officer. There was a Vulcan as Chief Engineering Officer and a Coridan alpha as Communications Officer. The ship's crew was about 1 percent Vulcan, 16 percent Tellarian, 14 percent Coridan alphas, 26 percent Rigellians, 23 percent Andorian, and 20 percent of Earth lineage.

The tensions aboard were considerable. Although everyone worked hard at containing their emotions, gripes, and discontents, it was not really possible. In his autobiography, James Kirk likened it to those trivial things that can break up even love marriages: "You leave the cap off the toothpaste, she never cleans the sink; you snore, she hums at the oddest time. It is these tiny irritations which can build into great schisms. We tried, we really did. Rigellians simply cannot *stand* the "normal" body odor of a healthy human. Jareel—the nav officer—said we smelled like rotting circle-bird eggs. He apologized, knowing it was not our fault. He said that the Rigellian commander had considered cauterizing all olfactory sensors, knowing confinement with humans could be determinedly offensive." [Author's note: This was before the development of the Rigel Olfactor-9.]

Kirk continued, saying that the Andorians *breathed* in a way that irritated the Tellarians. "The Tellarians developed on a planet with a sixteen-hour day and to conform to the standard twenty-hour day adopted by the Federation was very difficult for them, thus they were often irritable. The Coridan alphas were slow. The Vulcan calm was taken as arrogance by the Andorians. And so on. Nothing really big, but just a series of minor causes and effects that directly affected ship performance."

The report by Prince Fiawol to Starfleet Command resulted in Ship Performance Order 283-5196, which set policy, limiting starship personnel to a 90/10 percent policy, with exceptions possible but difficult. The 10 percent was set as a *maximum*, and in truth, the reality was closer to 2 percent.

It was not anything as destructive nor as important as racial intolerance that prompted this policy. It was, as Admiral Byron Komack said, that "it is difficult enough for any two people of the *same* race to live and work together, sharing a common culture, the same biological heritage, and shared interests. Change even one of those factors—a good-natured, intelligent hard-working member of one race working and living beside a good-natured, intelligent, hard-working member of another race, not just with the minor differences of Terra's races or between Coridan alphas, betas, and gammas, but someone from a *totally* different genetic, cultural, societal, and technological background—and you have unintended tensions which are ruinous to efficient starship functioning."

This policy was very flexible in some areas, in that a number of ships were staffed by *volunteers*, which the psychocrats considered more highly motivated. The *Tutakai*, the *Yaan*, and the *Androcus* were heavy cruisers with volunteer crews, as were the destroyers *James Tannenbaum*, *Thomas Stern*, *Black Elk*, and *Holländer*. But it must be noted that both the *Perseus* and the *Hannifen*, staffed with non-policy volunteer crews, never were heard from again.

Excerpt, Kirk, by Areel Shaw, with Lawrence Van Cott:

Kirk's promotion from First Officer on the *El Dorado* to Commanding Officer of the *Saladin* was a major step in his career, and in his attitude toward himself. An unfortunate experience as a young lieutenant on his first mission, on the *Farragut*, had created a certain hidden insecurity in Jim Kirk that was not to surface for some time. (See Chapter Twelve.)

Kirk has written of his first time on the bridge of the *Saladin*, a MK-VIII, *Saladin* class destroyer:

"Heavy cruisers are *the* ships of Starfleet, but still,

there is something about your first ship, and something about your first command. You love them or hate them, but you never forget them. The *Farragut* was my testing ground as an officer; the *El Dorado* my testing ground as a diplomat; the *Saladin* my testing ground as a commanding officer, and the *Enterprise* my proving ground.

"The bridges of destroyers are smaller, but not much smaller than those on heavy cruisers. They have all the same functions, except that the larger ship has more of each. I kept my eyes down—I don't know why—until the turbolift doors slid back, then I raised them, taking it all in at once.

"The captain was Lieutenant Commander Leonard Konigsburg, who was transferring to the *Rigel Kentaurus* as First Officer. He was a heavy man, muscled and slow, but his mind was as quick as a cat. I saluted him and gave him the formal words of relief. He returned my salute and told me the ship was mine. We shook hands and he clapped my arm and left. It was all formality. The real hellos and good-byes had already happened.

"We were in orbit around Lieberman's World, with the scout ship *Ursa Major* on our starboard, to take him to his new ship in the Prantaris sector. Konigsburg had already made his personal and professional farewells, and we had had the ritual drinks in his cabin, with him filling in on the personnel files all those little things, but important things, that cannot go into any official dossier.

"Then the ship was mine. I wanted to sit down in the command chair and give the order to have the ship taken out of orbit on impulse engines, but I had to wait. It seemed like an hour but I'm sure it was only minutes before the Transporter Room reported than Lieutenant Commander L. Konigsburg had left the ship.

"Then it was truly mine. All mine. I gave the order, and we moved carefully out of the clutter and invisible orbits that net each civilized world. We set course for Wolcott-7423. It was an ordinary mission—show the flag on a world making rumblings about seceding from the Federation. No real action was anticipated, nor was it desired by Starfleet.

"A milk run at Warp 5. Nothing important, nothing like sailing the wine-dark seas with Ulysses, nothing new, nothing special, just my first order as commanding officer.

"My first ship.

"My first command.

"No Saurean brandy is quite so heady."

Entry, dated 6 August 2167, from Diary, by Janice Rand Dale:

There seems to be a wall between JTK and myself. I can't break it down. Only he can do that. I'm a yeoman, he's a *captain*, with so many responsibilities. But he needs a woman; if not me, then someone!

THE GIFT OF LOVE

The gift of love is mine to make,
to child or man, jade or rake.
A gift of love is a loving thing,
built from what you to it bring.

This gift of love is the gift I give,
to a shy brave heart, to make him live.
I feel this life, racing past,
is much too swift for one love's task.

Excerpt, Supplementary Entry, Ship's Log, U.S.S. Enterprise, NCC-1701; Captain James T. Kirk, Commanding; dated 3045.6:

We arrived at Cestus III and found that the Federation base there, a harmless agrarian community directed by the Federation Department of Agriculture, had been destroyed by an alien race we had not previously encountered.

We followed the ion trail into an uncharted region of Sector 9/34-9a. There the ship was captured in an energy net that we could not break. Subsequent development revealed that our captors were a godlike race called the Metrons, who disliked trespassers and who seemed to hold all other races in distain, if not outright contempt.

They believed that physical combat was more suitable for individuals, rather than groups, and were preparing for combat with the alien vessel.

Excerpt, Science Officer Log, U.S.S. Enterprise, NCC-1701; Commander Spock recording, dated 3045.6:

. . . The Metrons stated that the winner of the individual combat contest would have his ship freed; the loser and his crew and ship would be destroyed. I did not find this a equitable solution; however, temporarily matters were out of my effective control.

Captain Kirk vanished from the bridge, to appear on the surface of an uninhabited asteroid which they had roughly terra-formed into an desertlike landscape of approximately equal discomfort to both Captain Kirk and the creature they placed opposite him. We identified the creature as the opposing starship captain, a mature Gorn.

The Gorn are intelligent but highly belligerent, and resemble a two-meter [seven-foot] reptile, not dissimilar to a Terran tyrannosaurus, a Vulcan *scal*, or a Vegan *sicanosaur*. The events to follow we monitored on our view screens throughout the *Enterprise*, a solution which was convenient but which gave me great concern about the integrity of our defensive screens.

The Gorn was indeed the one who had destroyed the base on Cestus III, a most illogical act, as the colony there was undefended and productive. However, the Gorn considered it a hostile invasion into their territory.

The Gorn had the advantage of a natural armor and superior strength over Captain Kirk, but as a mature human in excellent condition, James Kirk was swifter in his reactions and in his ability to move.

Our resourceful commander kept out of the claws of the Gorn long enough to combine the local mineral resources—placed there as a subtle test by the Metrons—into a crude gunpowder. He managed to construct a very inefficient cannon and, with the use of a rocky projectile, wounded the Gorn.

Excerpt, Supplementary Entry, Ship's Log, U.S.S. Enterprise, NCC-1701, Captain James T. Kirk, Commanding; dated 3045.6:

. . . But I refused to kill the Gorn warrior-captain. I just couldn't have done that. I have always avoided any taking of life, except, I'm afraid, where my own life or the lives of others were involved. But I had defeated the Gorn captain; I had no need to kill him. I stated this in forceful terms to the Metrons, whose words seemed to be in our heads.

I fully expected some form of horrible retaliation. Thus I was surprised when the Metrons conceeded that there might be, after all, some hope for the human race. Both the Gorn and I were returned to our respective ships and the ships pressed into some sort of immediate spacewarp, appearing at considerable distance from the Metrons.

Starfleet Command Advisory Order #1525, dated 9 Nov 2167:

To all warp-drive vessel commanders:

Enter this into your navigation and computation computers with a Crimson Alert tab: YOU ARE ADVISED TO STAY A MINIMUM OF FOUR LIGHT-YEARS AWAY FROM SECTOR 9, SUB 3/76a-13. THIS IS CONSIDERED A DANGER AREA. (Signed) Fleet Admiral Gregory Calkins, commanding.

Entry, dated 14 November 2167, from Diary, by Janice Rand Dale:

Tsu-hsi[1] kids me constantly about my infatuation for JTK and I just have to keep my mouth shut. I

[1]Yeoman Rand's bunkmate, an Electrician 2nd class.

cannot compromise him in any way, either directly or indirectly. He is not only a Starfleet officer, but ship's captain. That comes first. I know that. Their ships come first to all starship commanders. I suppose it should not be any other way, really.

But there are times when I might wish it another way.

Entry, dated 2 January 2168 from Diary, by Janice Rand Dale:

> *This is life*
> *This is the heartbeat of you*
> *This is you, in my arms*
>
> *We are life*
> *We are the life we know*
> *We are a two-part love*
>
> *There is life*
> *There is life living in us*
> *There is a chain to the future*
>
> *You are life*
> *You are the death of loneliness*
> *You are the other part of me*

Excerpt, Where No Man Has Gone Before, The Autobiography of James T. Kirk:

There is glory in sadness and sadness in glory. The events which culminated in the disappearance of both Captain Willard Decker and the transformed Ilya were a mixture of both of these things.

In a long career in Starfleet I have never encountered quite such a mixture of emotions and thoughts. Starfleet—and I, personally—are saddened by the loss of such a fine young officer as Captain Decker, and by the loss of V'ger of the Deltan officer as well.

Yet, yet there is a strange and wonderful sort of glory in what happened. We can but imagine what the fusion of those two entities produced or became, or where they went.

But that is not all bad. There is a special kind of romance in mysteries. We can, all of us, *imagine* what the fusion of Decker, Ilya, and V'ger became. They are there, perhaps in some form inexplicable to us, perhaps in some symbiotic relationship, perhaps in some form and function we cannot possibly fathom.

Godspeed!

Excerpt, Memoirs, by Dr. Leonard McCoy:

I visited Jim Kirk during that time after the V'ger affair. We had gone on for some time in space and had a series of adventures I'm afraid paled somewhat in comparison to that experience. Oh, the *Enterprise* was fine, better than ever, in fact, much like a patient not only made healthy but made better by an experience.

But, in time, we were ordered back to Earth. The crew was dispersed here and there. My old sparring partner Spock took over the final assessment of cadets in his usual manner. Chekov was transferred to the *Nelson*. Dr. Chapel went to Vega for research there. Scott went on the Academy staff, chaffing as always at being out of action.

Sulu was on staff, too, until he wrangled a berth on the *Republic*. Uhura taught Emergency Communications for a while, then she, too, managed an assignment to the *Hornet*. Scott went aboard the *Yorktown* when Massoglia caught a minor radiation sickness.

And I plugged away, the only one stuck permanently with a staff job. Maybe it's different for doctors. We do the patch jobs, fixing up from the actions done by others. But it was Jim who seemed to suffer the most.

I know he wanted to get back into space. But, being the good officer he is, he also wondered if perhaps he wasn't getting just a bit too old for the job. Starship captains are young, at least by the standards of the old sailing ships and the first interplanetary vessels. Those pioneering astronauts were not teenagers, either.

I visited him at his San Francisco quarters when we were both on leave. We drank and reminisced and laughed, and I think he was both glad and sad to see me. Glad of the comradeship, glad of the memories we shared, and saddened, too, because it seemed to have come to an end.

"Maybe I won't get a ship," he said.

"Jim, you're valuable to Starfleet right where you are," I said. "How many ship's captains have been through what you've done, been where you've been? You've got to help those kids. It's a bizarre universe out there; you must give them a hand, a chance at survival."

He had nodded and said I was right, but I knew his heart was not in agreement. Men like Jim Kirk, they should die with their boots on, die on a strange world under a distant sun. To die of old age, on Earth, in a most ordinary way, that was not the proper finish for a man like Kirk.

Understand: he was not morbid, not sorry for himself, not suicidal, not angry. He said to me, "Bones, I remember once, when I was a young man, at college—the campus was still in Westwood then, though it hadn't looked like those postcard campuses in decades. I was driving to the beach at Malibu. Had a fine little Turboford. I saw this woman. I was sixteen, I guess. She was, oh, twenty. Had that kind of beauty that looks okay at first glance, better at second look, stunning at third, and you are in love at fourth."

"She looked at me. Our eyes met. She smiled. I was too dumb, too young, too *anything* to react. She was watering a lawn. Little strip of green in front of an arcolog. Blondish hair, blue jumper. I remember every detail."

"And?" I prompted.

"And the light changed, the air traffice started thundering by, I moved on and never saw her again."

"Jim, you've seen a lot of women since then."

"Yes, Bones, I know. I never knew her name, never saw her, never tried to find her. But I remember her."

"Ships that pass in the night," I said, trying to lighten it up. I poured him some wine.

"Missed opportunity. That's the way I feel now. The fleet's going on without me. I'm beached. A has-been."

I'm afraid I laughed. He glared at me for a second before he relaxed. "You'll never be a has-been, Jim," I said. "What you are is an individual in preparation to *be*."

"Be what?"

"Be *anything*. Look what you've gone through. You've done things no man has ever done before. You and Spock—you saved the *Earth*, Jim. V'ger was going to—"

He cut me short. He smiled ruefully. "But what have I done *lately?*"

I had no answer for that. We talked of other things, of old shipmates, of starships lost and starships returned, of Saurean brandy and tribbles, of shoes and ships and cabbages.

I left him long after midnight. We were both mellow, but there was an edge to his mood, a sadness.

Excerpt, Khan Noonian Singh: The Years in Exile, by Gene Wilbur:

We have very few facts to reconstruct the years spent in exile by this former prince of the Earth. His death in space, along with all his followers, closed us off forever from factual reconstruction. The planetoid formed from the wreckage of the *Reliant* and from hydrogen atoms swept in from a vast cubic area of space, leaves no clues.[1]

But Starfleet issued a report[2] of their examination of the Khan survival colony on Ceti Alpha V, and I summarize their official prose here.

The shifting of Ceti Alpha V into its new orbit

swept away most of the atmosphere, put vast amounts of dust into the air, and created a turbulence within the remaining biosphere that will last for centuries. "Perhaps permanently, like Jupiter," Dr. Gail Shulman suggested. "The orbital speed was altered, the rotation period increased by about 18 percent and the axial tilt increased by 5.4 percent."

In layman's terms, the planet was wrecked. It would be eons before any sort of stable environment might be produced.

The Starfleet report said that the primitive shelter created from rock, bits of shale, and portions of the planetary ship that had been wrecked was indeed a great comedown for a man who had once lived in palaces, drunk the finest of wines, eaten the best of foods, and had about him the genetic "cream of the crop."

The report stated: "The survivors had lived on short rations, and their underground food-generating 'farms' had frequent failures because of a deteriorating generator supplying power to the 'fast-gro' lights. The water supply was polluted physically with sand and biologically with *coris* bacillae. Only human beings with a superior immunologic system could have lived past the first months."

Elsewhere the report suggests that a portion of the surviving population had been rendered sterile by their bodies' constant fight against the diseases running loose.

Water was a constant problem. Severe ruptures of the rock mantle of Ceti Alpha V had caused underground water to come to the surface, but subsequent ruptures had drained most of it away. Water, according to the Federation scientists, was obtained only by a dangerous route underground, in almost total darkness, through frequently collapsing rents in the rock, and a nest of Ceti eels. The water was transported in makeshift waterskins of tough plastic crating material, a myriad of small capped containers, and a single primitive waterskin.

"Life on Ceti Alpha V," wrote Dr. Shulman in her summation, "must have been more difficult than we can imagine. Only Khan's genetically designed creatures could have borne the adversity. This must have fed on Khan's mind constantly, driving him into monomania concerning his old adversary, Captain James Kirk."

[1]This planetoid has been given the designation Ceti Alpha VII by Starfleet, but the popular press is already calling it Khan.

[2]*Starfleet Special Report 11-008-B6, "Investigation of Ceti Alpha V,"* authorized by Starfleet Command.

Letter, Dr. David Marcus to Dr. Carol Marcus, dated 2 April 2168:

Dear Mother:

I wanted you to know my further thoughts on what we discussed aboard the *Enterprise*. As I said then, I understood your reasons for keeping me from my biological father. You had your world and he had his. Both are unique and can only touch in the most tangential of fashions. The first of those "touchings" produced me, the second was of great benefit to humankind.

Although I can only praise your efforts throughout my life to be both mother and father to me, to deny certain needs within yourself to care for me, I can say now that I am most happy to acknowledge James Kirk as my father, and to rejoice in his acknowledgment of me.

I know that you asked him not to interfere, to, in effect, remove us from his memory. But he exists in me, as I exist in you, and we cannot successfully deny that, whatever the subsequent feelings.

I'm proud now to be the son of James Kirk. Not because of his great rank and fame, for you know my feeling toward the quasimilitary aspects of Starfleet, although I acknowledge their necessity. I'm proud to be his son—and *your* son—and trust that I shall live up to the standards I perceive in both of you. I am proud to be the son of James Kirk because he is a special kind of person who accepts the responsibility, not only for his own life, but for the life of his crew, and, indirectly, the lives and well-being of the billions who live under the law of the Federation.

To hold the loyalty of such as Spock, Dr. McCoy, Engineer Scott, yourself, and others, one must be a special kind of person. I hope, someday, to be that kind of person, one of strength and trust and honesty.

All my life I had been denying him, fighting against what I *thought* he was. I suppose that, in that, I am no different from billions of other sons throughout history. We perceive our father and our mother in ways that are perhaps untrue, or misleading. To have seen him in action, to have seen his strength, imagination, and almost intuitive decision-making is to see why he commands respect— not because of his rank, but because of *him*.

Now I may see him more clearly but, in truth, perhaps simply through a different set of rose-colored glasses, as the ancient adage goes.

I thank you for selecting him to be my father, and someday, circumstances permitting, I shall thank him for knowing you, however briefly.

Your son, David

McCoy, Leonard Edward

SERIAL NUMBER: MD398-1214

PRESENT RANK: Commander
BORN: Atlanta, Georgia, Terra, 24 Oct 2119
FATHER: Robert Edward Lee McCoy
MOTHER: Maureen Abney
SIBLINGS:
>Henry Clay McCoy
>(Leonard Edward McCoy)
>Landor Abney McCoy
>Melissa Jane McCoy
>Elizabeth Ashley McCoy

MARITAL STATUS: Married: Elinor Lee, 10 October 2148; Divorced: 3 December 2153.
CHILDREN: Joanna Lee McCoy
EDUCATION: Primary/Secondary Schools, Atlanta, Georgia, Terra; University of Georgia; John Hopkins University; *Internship:* John Hopkins, Luna Special Laboratory; Interstellar Medical Institute, Alpha Centauri II.
PRIMARY LANGUAGE: English; also Universal English, minor in French
COMMENDATIONS:
>Commendation (informal) by the Empath of Minara
>Commendation by the Government of Dramaia for "significant achievement in the field of interstellar medicine" for the cure to auroral plague.
>Starfleet United Citation, with Two Clusters
>Vega Award of Merit, Star Class
>United Federation of Planets Hippocrates Award
>Starfleet Commendations: 14

AWARDS OF VALOR:
>Silver Palm with Cluster
>Legion of Honor
>Federation Exceptional Service Medal
>United Federation of Planets Golden Sun with Star
>Starfleet Citation for Conspicuous Gallantry

CRYOSURGICAL FRAME RATING: One

INTERESTS: Medical history; the 1860–65 Civil War of the
    United States of America; Saurian brandy;
    Xenobiology and Physiology

STARFLEET ASSIGNMENTS:

Memory Alpha, Assistant Medical Officer

U.S.S. *Crockett*, NCC-600 (Scout Ship), Medical
    Officer

U.S.S. *Xerxes*, NCC-505 (Destroyer), Medical Officer

U.S.S. *Al Mahdi*, NCC-545 (Destroyer) Chief Medical
    Officer

U.S.S. *Tajarhi*, NCC-1783 (Heavy Cruiser) Chief
    Medical Officer

U.S.S. *Lafayette*, NCC-1720 (Heavy Cruiser), Chief
    Medical Officer

Starfleet Academy, staff

U.S.S. *Enterprise*, NCC-1701 (Heavy Cruiser), Chief
    Medical Officer

Starfleet Academy, staff

U.S.S. *Enterprise*, NCC-1701 (Heavy Cruiser), Chief
    Medical Officer

Starfleet Academy, staff

U.S.S. *Enterprise*, NCC-1701 (Heavy Cruiser), Chief
    Medical Officer

Excerpt, Memoirs, by Dr. Leonard McCoy:

In writing this volume of memories, I came across
an entry in my diary, barely readable from its years
of lying dormant in the heart of a molecule, abraded
by electrons, flecked with static, and in a form of
personal code I barely remembered.

"I long for space," I had entered into the memory
bank. "It is the final mystery before death. Earth is

so static, so ordinary. The grass is green, the sky is blue, there are no surprises."

I was twelve years old when I wrote that. My father was off on what proved to be his final five-year voyage. My mother had stayed behind, limiting her practice to care for my sisters and brothers, getting infrequent subspace messages and dreading the day when two officers of rank equal to or superior to my father might come up the walk with solemn faces to tell us of some accident on some world we had never heard of or of some encounter with a deadly race of intelligent worms or some such bizarre ending.

When I was a bit past thirteen I wrote this: "I must go into space. It is my destiny." This was set into a block of stars, so I must have considered it important, though I do not remember writing it.

I do remember the feeling, however. The longing for the stars, the freedom and excitement it meant. I remember wondering why man had not just kept on going after the first steps on the moon. Had they not realized the riches, the wonder, the knowledge that lay beyond our rather unimportant little star system? The fact that it was years between the primitive Apollo program and even that Wright Brothers–style Space Shuttle is astonishing. Today, looking back, it seems suicidal. We came so *very* close to not getting off the planet at all that it is frightening.

But we did and I did, and I suppose this memoir reflects that. I am not the adventurer like Jim Kirk, nor the coldly logical accomplisher of miracles of a Spock, but I too ached for the stars. And am grateful I found them.

Excerpt, Memoirs, by Dr. Leonard McCoy:

At first, my assignment to the *Enterprise* was simply that, an assignment to another heavy cruiser. I really hadn't cared much one way or another where they sent me, as long as it was *away*. The divorce from Elinor had been messy and destructive and I had spent several years avoiding Earth. I had drifted after leaving the Interstellar Medical Institute on Alpha Centauri II, taking a trading ship to this and that distant world, doing my job, until one day I helped out the medical officer on the *Crockett* and saw how they did things and how much they *cared*.

It made me face myself and what I saw I did not much like. I was drinking too much and while I thought I was just as good a doctor as ever, I realized that fine edge was off. It was a disturbing revelation and one which hounded me for four months.

At the end of that time we were in the Santarus sector and my contract was up. Instead, I volunteered for Starfleet. They sent me to *Memory Alpha* as an assistant medical officer. In the next few years I was assigned to starships—my first assignment to replace the medical officer on the *Crockett!*—then to other ships. It was interesting and valuable work and my sense of wonder about the beauty and intricacy of the human body returned.

During this time I often thanked the stars that I had not become the drunk I might have. I still like to drink, but now it is a pleasant social experience, rather than the dark tunnel into which I disappeared to forget Elinor, youthful dreams, my daughter and everything else.

Why I chose the stars instead of some remote South Pacific island to romantically disintregate is simple: the stars are in my blood. My maternal great-grandfather had shipped as M.O. on the *Armstrong* to Alpha Centauri,; my grandmother on my father's side had been an M.O. on the *Andrea Byrne* during the Romulan war and was killed at the Battle of Starbase Eleven.

Letter, Dr. Joseph Boyce, M.D., to Captain James T. Kirk, U.S.S. Enterprise, dated 1513.2:

Dear Jim:

I just heard you have Leonard McCoy as your C.M.O. He's a good man. I first met him when he was A.M.O. on *Memory Alpha,* and he was a great help in the research I was doing then on Vegan mind cramp. I later ran into him on the *Xerxes,* when I was deadheading from Beta Epsilon III back to Luna. Tell him he lost his bet about Nurse Staton and owes me a flask of Saurian.

But I really just wanted to tell you you can rely on him. Listen to him. All you starship honchos are the same—you think you know everything. Well, you don't, not about medical matters, so *listen.* You may have been the fair-haired lad, going into Starfleet Academy at an early age (I shipped with Dr. Stewart Baumgard on the *Altair* and he Told All) but Leonard McCoy was just as much a prodigy as you, Captain Sir.

Now tell him this: Don't run the holisticon past the 1000 mark without a good warmup. (Remember, I used to be on the *Enterprise?)* He'll know what I mean.

Good luck on your voyage! Stock up on a lot of leeches and sugar pills for McCoy!

Excerpt, "Introduction," Xenobiology, by Dr. Leonard McCoy:

Space is stranger than fiction. Lifeforms exist that seem impossible. The bizarre and strange are common, so common that the more familiar forms of plant and animal life seem to be the weird ones.

If the amazing variety of mutations that occured during evolution of life on Earth seem vast, they are but a drop in any sea compared to the variety to be seen in a single star system.

The copper-based green blood of the noble Vulcan race seems almost brotherly compared to the strange forms of intelligent and nonintelligent life I encountered on my two voyages aboard the U.S.S. *Enterprise*, which is the basis of my research for this book.

I was priviledged to be a part of that team which did so much to open up the unknown vastness of our galaxy to human exploration. Under the command of the finest starship captain I have ever known, James T. Kirk, and with the help, knowledge, and critical assistance of our Science Officer, Commander Spock, I was a part of that great adventure, still ongoing and never ceasing, of the exploration of space.

But it is to my Chief Nurse, Christine Chapel, that I dedicate this book. Without her assistance, support, and friendship I might not have been able to survive the incredible and demanding rigors of the early voyage. All of us who were aboard the *Enterprise* know what we owe her.

Excerpt, The Voyages of the U.S.S. Enterprise, by John Griffin:

On the ancient sailing ship of Earth's ocean the radio operator was often called "Sparks" and the medical doctor—when they had one—was frequently called "Bones." Thus it was on the *Enterprise*, when Captain Kirk dubbed Leonard McCoy with that affectionate nickname.

In the years of the first voyage under Kirk, Dr. McCoy distinguished himself numerous times. He developed the antidote to counteract the inhibition-relaxing virus of Psi-2000, which had totally wrecked the discipline of the landing party.

He is credited with advances in the Feinberger scanner (suggested to the Ship's Engineer and physically done by Commander Scott), and his suggestions on the expansion of sensors for the standard diagnostic panel are still in use today. His antidote for the Saurian virus alone would have given him a place in the medical history of space exploration.

During an interview by INS after the second defeat of Khan, Dr. McCoy was quoted as saying this: "I am not a medical pioneer in the tradition of Ehrlich, Lister, Fleming, or Pasteur. I'm more like Walter Reed, if I can make so bold a comparison. I'm on the spot. Lives depend on me finding a solution. I do not have the luxury of a laboratory on safe ground, of meditation, time, and Federation grants.

"I'm the man on the spot. I must make, all too

often, guesses. We all make guesses, right back to Hippocrates. We are all guessing beyond known facts, extrapolating upon very little known and proven fact. But I cannot have the luxury of operating on an unlimited time frame, of tests and more tests, of test subjects even. The ship, the lives of the crew, and sometimes even the lives of everyone in human space depends upon my decisions, right or wrong, and upon other Chief Medical Officers in other ships throughout the galaxy.

"I have a great staff on the *Enterprise*, but they are just as fallible as I am. I make mistakes. The trick is to learn from the mistakes and, of course, to make as few as possible.

"When you have the kind of medical problems we encountered, you cannot do work As Usual. You must allow your mind to run loose, to explore beyond the normal boundaries of your thinking routine, to go past the inhibitions of your training and culture.

"We are just one race out there, we Terrans; even the Vulcans are a rather harsh version of *Homo sapiens*. But we encountered creatures of great intelligence, creatures whose body chemistry was beyond belief, beings who were pure energy, beings who sailed the void like stardust, intelligences beyond our capacity to understand.

"My advice to any starship medical officer is this: Look beyond the obvious, yet do not be blind to the obvious.

"Space is the ultimate strangeness, the ultimate adventure, the ultimate challenge."

Excerpt, Kirk, by Areel Shaw, with Lawrence Van Cott:

Spock had become very strange, and Dr. McCoy told Captain Kirk that unless they went to Vulcan, Spock would die. Kirk took it upon himself to divert the *Enterprise* from its mission and go to Vulcan. Spock invited Kirk and McCoy down to the planet to participate in a marriage ceremony: his. In childhood they discovered Vulcans of the higher class were married. It was a ritual that is actually "less than a marriage, but more than a bethrothal." The minds of two participants were locked together at age seven. At the proper time in adulthood they are drawn to *Koon-ut kai-if-fee,* the Vulcan term for marriage, which also means "challenge."

If the marriage is challenged at that time, the two competing males fight to the death, since the biological forces controlling a Vulcan male when he is in *pon far,* the "mating time," are completely out of his power to suppress or control. The Vulcan male will then go into *plak tow,* a blood frenzy.

To all Vulcans this is an embarrassing and shameful emotional state for which they had never been able to find a cure, either mental or physical.

It is with this background that we present this excerpt.

T'Pring was an astonishingly beautiful woman, according to Dr. McCoy. "And I don't mean *for a Vulcan,* but for any humanoid race. Truly stunning— but headstrong and quite powerful in her own way. It was obvious she preferred another Vulcan, Stonn, a burly fellow who wasn't traveling all over the stars but staying right at home, where T'Pring wanted her husband."

Thus the marriage was challenged, and by ancient Vulcan law Spock must fight. T'Pring made it quite clear she preferred Stonn, and Stonn was quite ready to fight to the death for what Kirk later called "the pearl of Vulcan beauty." But T'Pring was more devious than any had anticipated. She saw the friendship between Spock and Kirk, and chose Kirk as her champion. Kirk accepted, knowing that Spock was quite debilitated from his ordeal prior to coming to Vulcan. He said at a later date, "I thought to throw the fight. Then they told me the snapper: the fight was to the death."

The heat of Vulcan was intense, and during the first bout the atmosphere and heat had quite reduced Captain Kirk's ability to fight. Dr. McCoy protested. "It was sapping him terribly. I had trouble breathing. I argued with T'Pau about injecting Jim with a tri-ox compound to compensate."

T'Pau, who had arrived to officiate over the ceremony, is herself an extraordinary character. She is an ancient and venerable Vulcan matriarch with immense prestige, the only person to ever refuse a seat in the Federation Council. Kirk said later, "I didn't realize how important Spock's family—Sarek and Amanda—were until I recognized T'Pau. It would be something like the King of England coming to your wedding, only more so."

McCoy said, "She saw the disadvantage Jim suffered and agreed to the tri-ox, and the second round began."

The fight resumed . . . and Captain James T. Kirk died.

Dr. McCoy sadly took the body back to the *Enterprise* for burial in space. Mr. Spock's shock at killing not only his captain, but his best friend, expunged the mating urge from his system. With a clear head, Spock saw the reality of his situation, and surrendered T'Pring to Stonn, her real interest. He returned to the ship and immediately placed himself under arrest for killing his commanding officer. But the final surprise was the Vulcan's, for Kirk was *not* dead!

Dr. McCoy had given Kirk a knockout drug instead of the tri-ox compound and had adjusted the setting on his Feinberger scanner to show no life readings.

"There was a second there," McCoy said, "when I thought that Vulcan was human. Just a second, mind you. You might even call it a second of unrestrained rejoicing. It was like a flash of lightning on a hot Georgia summer night. Then he was back to the same stoic old Vulcan."

Captain Kirk in his autobiography said, "I was never certain that T'Pau did not know what was going on, what McCoy was up to or what he did. Perhaps it was her way of fixing things. But, on the other hand, if McCoy hadn't done *something*, I'm afraid the *Enterprise* would have needed a new captain."

Excerpt, Offworld, by Hikaru Sulu and B. J. O'Katwin:

Stardate: 5476.3.

Dr. McCoy received perhaps the most devastating news any person can receive: his death notice. Facing the possibility of death is one thing. Advancing under fire, taking a calculated risk, betting your life, as risky as all these things are, there is a portion of it that says "life." But when you receive a valid medical report that says you have an incurable blood disease and the time limit of approximately one year, it must be the most horrible of news.

At that same time, the *Enterprise* encountered an asteroid far out in space. We subsequently learned it was called Yonada, and was artifically propelled. We discovered life-form readings and found that there was a hollow center, inhabited by humanoids within .4 of *Homo sapiens* norm.

They had been sent as a "seed ship" into space to perpetuate their race on some distant, unknown planet. These humanoids were not in cryogenic suspension; this was a "generation" ship. Over several hundred years they had lost vital information and did not even realize they were on a ship. Even the concept of "ship" was unknown to them.

The difficulty was that the asteroid was on a collision course with a Federation planet. We discovered that the controls had been damaged and that a simple alteration in course was impossible.

These asteroid people were ruled by Natira, a priestess who took orders from her "god" and did not realize it was an advanced computer. While Mr. Spock and Captain Kirk were hunting for a way into the central computer, Dr. McCoy fell in love.

We all realized later that the "death sentence" given our beloved "Bones" had released him from the strictures of Starfleet discipline, even from his older discipline of medicine. He seemed quite willing to stay there with the beautiful priestess Natira, living out his last days.

At that point Natira ordered Mr. Spock and the Captain back aboard the *Enterprise* for having broken some of Yonada's laws. But McCoy stayed behind, married Natira, and accepted the implant of the Instrument of Obedience, which punished dissent, into his body.

Not long after, McCoy, perhaps in memory of his friendship with Captain Kirk, used his communicator to call the *Enterprise* and tell him he might have found the secret controls, but then he was struck down by the electronic device in his body. Mr. Spock and Captain Kirk transported back into the asteroid's hollow center and removed the Instrument of Obedience, freeing "Bones."

They were unable to truly convince Natira they were *inside* a spaceship of rock. They did make their way into the heart of the computer—but not without a fight! They put Yonada back upon the original course, and I helped realign the self-guidance mechanism that would allow the asteroid the advantage of avoidance maneuvers.

Mr. Spock found a cure for Dr. McCoy's disease, and the doctor reluctantly returned to the *Enterprise*, his life now extended into that strange unknown we all face.

Natira remained behind, the marriage dissolved, to guide her people. I remember her last words to McCoy. "Perhaps, someday, if it is permitted, you will again find your Yonada."

Scott, Montgomery

SERIAL NUMBER: SE197-514

PRESENT RANK: Commander
BORN: Aberdeen, Scotland, Terra, 31 August 2121
FATHER: Robert Burns Scott
MOTHER: Mary Darnley
SIBLINGS:
James McNeil Scott
(Montgomery Scott)
Mary Darnley Scott
MARITAL STATUS: Unmarried
CHILDREN: None
EDUCATION: Primary and secondary schools Edinburgh,
Scotland, Terra; University of Edinburgh, Scotland,
Terra; Starfleet Academy, Class 81
STARFLEET ACADEMY GRADE AVERAGE: 3.7
PRIMARY LANGUAGE: English; Also Universal English,
Celtic, minor in German
COMMENDATIONS:
Prantares Ribbob of Commendation, First Class
Vega Award of Merit, Star Class
United Federation of Planet Golden Sun with Oak
Leaf
Starfleet Unit Citation, with Three Clusters
Starfleet Commendations: 67
AWARDS OF VALOR:
Silver Palm with Cluster
Coridan Order of Heroism
Miradi Empire Order of Courage
Trexlor Silver Disc
Axanar Medal with Lightning Bolt
Blantar Award of Merit with Silver Astroid
Legion of Honor
Federation Exceptional Service Medal
Starfleet Citation for Conspicuous Gallantry
United Federation of Planets Golden Sun
CONDEMNATIONS: None
STARFLEET DEMERITS: Six

INTERESTS: Machinery; collects samples of alcoholic
  beverages such as Sirian *belisk*, Coridan beer, Triacus
  pod wine, Saurian brandy, Andorian wine-analog
  Vegan aromatic, Troyan mead, Rigellian *dorf* whiskey,
  Trora (from Eminiar VII especially), Antarean brandy,
  and Centaurian swamp-sweet.

STARFLEET ASSIGNMENTS:

U.S.S. *Constitution*, NCC-1117 (Heavy Cruiser),
  Assistant Engineering Officer

U.S.S. *Hood*, NCC-1703 (Heavy Cruiser), Assistant
  Engineering Officer

U.S.S. *Coridan Queen*, NCC-561 (Destroyer), Chief
  Engineering Officer

U.S.S. *Steven Barnes*, NCC-559 (Destroyer), Chief
  Engineering Officer

U.S.S. *Enterprise*, NCC-1701 (Heavy Cruiser), Chief
  Engineering Officer

Starfleet Academy, staff

U.S.S. *Enterprise*, NCC-1701 (Heavy Cruiser), Chief
  Engineering Officer

U.S.S. *Yorktown*, NCC-1704 (Heavy Cruiser), Chief
  Engineering Officer

U.S.S. *Enterprise*, NCC-1701 (Heavy Cruiser), Chief
  Engineering Officer

**Excerpt, letter from Midshipman Montgomery Scott to
Robert and Mary Scott, dated 16 April 2144:**

. . . And tell Mary the tests were hard, but I passed.
I seem to have that touch, with machinery of every
kind. Remember how the lads brought me their
handcomps to fix, and the time I repaired Reverend
McKenzie's Bible reader?

I know I'll feel at home. Or will, once I can get out

into space. (I don't count the Moon—I'm talking of *Deep* Space!) There is so much more to see, to do, to find!

I hope to find a posting to the *Constitution*. Have Jamie pull it up on the console for you. A bonny ship! A great ship, with more being built in that class all the time. It's a rare good thing the solar energy stations survived that last foolish little skirmish. Cheap energy is our wealth, letting the Federation grow and prosper.

They're expensive, these starships, but I hear the new spacewarp drive tests are running fine. That means, however, we can go anywhere! The old warp ships were marvels in their day, but the Warp II drives are vastly better! Those old ships have been putting us out into the stars for decades, but we can do now in weeks what it took them *years* to do! I'm certainly living at the right time. With a faster-than-light speed we can go everywhere, see everything!

Tell Jamie I don't mind him finding that wee bottle of Glenlivet I had stashed away. He put it to a fine use—if she decides to marry the monster, I'll find a case for him!

Excerpt, Scott, the Story of a Spaceman, by Lisa Araminta:

There was perhaps no man of his time who was more eager to get into space. Although his affinity for machinery of every kind, including that of non-human origin, has been lauded time and again, it must be pointed out that this was not at all unusual. Starfleet had the "pick of the litter," and these engineers were of a breed.

Where Montgomery Scott was perhaps somewhat different was in his determination to overcome all obstacles, no matter how large, in his desire to "get into space," as the phrase of the day had it.

Excerpt, Trek to the Stars; The Story of Human Exploration, by Christopher Lloyd:

There was a straining at the leash in those times, an eagerness to go beyond the frustrating limits set by the speed of light. It was rightfully considered a kind of magic, a quantum leap beyond the boundaries set by time, energy, and dimension.

The building of the great ships was an ongoing source of news. There were at one time no less than nineteen electronic magazines devoted solely to various aspects of starship development. Fanciful plays were made on what man might find once he had overcome the Newtonian limits, once he had leaped beyond the implacable wall set by Einstein.

Schools and colleges throughout Earth offered courses in many aspects of what was believed to be needed by these first explorers. The accomplishments of those pioneers who set out in "sleeper ships" for the United Federation of Planets on an almost weekly basis were forgotten in the great flood of excitement that attended the final tests of a space-warp drive.

Excerpt, "Introduction," Basic Starship Design, by Stephen Tolliver:

"One small step for a man, one giant leap for mankind." Those were the words of Neil Armstrong, putting a booted foot on the single natural satellite of Terra so long ago. It was not until Zefrem Cochrane announced that a practical faster-than-light drive had been tested and found workable, that Mankind did truly take that giant leap.

Letter, Midshipman Montgomery Scott to Mary Scott; dated 4 Mar 2145:

It's happening, lassie! Out at the San Francisco Navy Yard they're forming the first bit of keel for a starship that will carry the stardrive! Imagine! The *Bonaventure* proved out fine, as I'm sure ye know by now, and they are putting this new one together in orbit. It's a grand day!

The new one, by the way, will be the *Enterprise*, but the ship I want is the *Constitution*—she's the first, they've named the whole class after her. Wish me luck on getting aboard after graduation, because the *Connie's* set for a warp drive right after this *Enterprise* thing.

Excerpt, letter from Ensign Montgomery Scott to Robert and Mary Scott, undated:

I thank ye for coming all the way to the ceremony. It meant a lot. I'm glad you liked me mates, though I admit, as Mother said, they are a hard-drinking lot. We are all looking forward to pub crawling on some star you can't even see from here!

But here's the news: I'm posted to the *Constitution!* I'll be helping to install the new Warp-II engines, then we do some testing—just a wee jaunt out to Pluto and around Jupiter and back, then over to Alpha Centauri.

Won't that be a surprise for old Uncle Malcolm! All that way, all that time, and his own grand-nephew is waiting at the dock, as it were! We think the sleeper ship and the *Constitution* will arrive about the same time. McPhearson says it's a public-ity gimmick—the sleeper and the warp drive ship, side by side—but I don't care.

I'm to be Second Assistant Engineering Officer. If you want to write me, the ship number is NCC–1017. We'll be in construction orbit until July, and after that the only communication will be by subwarp radio and that's far too expensive.

Letter, Ensign Montgomery Scott to Margaret Bane, of Edinburgh; dated 19 April 2146:

Bonnie lass, I've been posted, I have. The *Constitu-tion*, and a grand ship she is! I'm First Assistant Engineering Officer, a certain Mr. Alexander being too confident of a drinking bout with an unnamed young Scot and arriving ten hours late. I meant no harm to the lad, you see, but he should not have had such misplaced confidence in the alleged superior abilities of a mere Englishman.

It's a great challenge, and I hope you understand that I won't be able to write as often in the near future, as I will be truly busy. I hope you keep that smile going for me.

Excerpt, letter from Ensign Montgomery Scott to Robert and Mary Scott, dated 18 December 2146:

. . . and tell Jamie you never saw such sights, not even if you had watched television all your life, not even if you stood on a highest hill in the heath. The stars are all around you, top, bottom, out as far as you can see.

They're colored all the colors there are; faint but very much there. When you go into warp drive they blur and run as if some god had made them of watercolor paint.

There's no sensation, just the usual thrum and hum of the ship, of the great bonnie engines that drive her. You just start moving, faster and faster, with incredible speed, swifter than anything but rumor.

There's been only one disappointment. I knew in me heart that Jupiter and Saturn were not as brightly colored as all those pictures we've seen, but somehow those were the images I had of these great gas planets. They're not like that at all. Rather dull, really, in comparison. But don't let a bit of computer enhancement slow things down. Space is where it is all happening now! It's like being in the sixteenth century, with a New World opening up. And these *are* worlds, not just a couple of continents.

I know, in a way, I'm a johnny-come-lately to space. No denying that. Sleeper ships have been sending out people for two hundred years! There are colonies and everything, springing up all over. And all the other planets in the Federation, they've been out building even longer than we have.

But this is *my* first time, *my* first voyages, and everything is new! Pray for me.

Excerpt, A Short History of the United Federation of Planets, by Elizabeth Palmer:

Earthmen ran into the stars as if escaping something. Their energy—and, often, their ruthlessness—appalled and frightened some of the more peaceful planets. They sensed they had loosed either a great plague or a great blessing on the universe.

Earthmen were new, untried, unknown, but strong, imaginative, and swift to react to new situations. It was the hallmark of those earth Terrans that they—to use a term of the period—"hustled."

Letter, Margaret Bane to Ensign Montgomery Scott, dated 1 June 2148:

Scotty, I've found another man. We're getting married as soon as he gets his next promotion. It's not that I didn't love you, my darling, it's just that you are so like every spaceman and woman I've met: you are in love with the stars, with your ship, and with what lies beyond the next star.

I need a man here, where I can touch him at night and where he can see the children growing up. He's a good man, a steady man, and he knows about you. He's a bit jealous, I think . . . well, more than a bit . . . and thinks you are running off to get away from our problems here. The government is raising taxes, the new television season is all starships and pratfalls, the pipes are old, my mother's artificial kidney has gone bad, and the medical insurance is dragging its feet.

His name is Duncan, Edgar Duncan, and we're to be married on the sixteenth of August in the chapel where my mother and father were wed. We're taking the shuttle to Lunaport for our honeymoon—a terrible extravagance, but maybe the last chance I'll have to see space as you see it. Mayhap I'll see what you see in it.

I hope you find someone, besides them engines of yours you've been writing so gloriously about.

Your Maggie—habit, I guess. *Once* your Maggie

Excerpt, A Scottish Lad Goes to the Stars, by Robert Braffyll Shaw:

Scott mounted a monumental drunk in a bar called *The Sleeping Dog*, in New Houston [on Alpha Centauri IV]. His shipmates said they were astounded at not only the quantity consumed but the ferocity with which he drank.

It was the unfortunate luck of a group of local citizens to take exception to Scott singing the national anthem of Scotland. The brawl, according to recorded accounts, lasted most of an hour before military police found their way to this swampside bar. The fight did not cease but merely expanded, to include the MPs, two crewmen off a Rigellian ship, seven to ten Andorians, and at least one Tellurite, plus several of the *Constitution* crew.

Scott was not reprimanded, as he was not arrested, due to the early unconscious state of the two Military Police, rendered so by person or persons unknown. The *Constitution* took a four-hour-early leave without Ensign Scott's ever contacting an uncle who was due to arrive via sleeper ship about that time.

Letter from Lieutenant Scott to Robert and Mary Scott, undated:

You'll please note the new rank, as well deserved a promotion as the Fleet has ever awarded, you can be certain.

And I've a new assignment, the *Hood* (NCC–1703), a fine ship bound for (they say, they say, they *say*) Andor. The ships are going everywhere these days—just as I predicted—and we humans are making our mark!

Tell Jamie I've found a new substance, Rigelian whiskey. It tastes like copper tacks going down, but like a rainbow in your head.

Citation, Starfleet Command: Recommended by Captain Hojo Yorii, dated 11 August 2151:

It is in the highest tradition of Starfleet that I commend Lieutenant Montgomery Scott, SE197-514, for conspicuous gallantry, 1469.2, during an engagement with a Klingon vessel of the Kangor Class. He maintained engine performance during battle despite the injury and later death of the Chief Engineering Officer and severe damage to the stern baffle panels and sensory array. His performance was an inspiration to the Engineering Section and a credit to the U.S.S. *Hood*.

Signed: Hojo Yorii, Captain, commanding

Letter, Lt. Montgomery Scott to his parents, dated 1469.7:

Promotion! I'll be sorry to leave the *Hood*, she's a good ship and the captain is TBF (Tough-But-Fair, to you with mud on your feet!). It's a Destroyer-class ship, the *Coridan Queen*—the name is an obvious attempt by the Federation to flatter that system into joining up—and she's no *Constitution* class. But you will note and brag to all the neighbors (particularly that Mrs. Byrne who thought I'd be killed in a bar on Luna) that I am now *Chief* Engineering Officer, a man to be reckoned with and never to be crossed by man or captain, once I'm in my hold.

Excerpt, Starfleet's Other Ships, by Dian Ardmore Crain:

While all the glory has gone to the big ships, the magnificent *Constitution*-class beauties who sailed into the unknown, who extended the mind and reach of man far beyond the known stars, we should not forget the service done also by the smaller ships, the *Argos* and *Defender* and *Coridan Queen*, the *Reiko Izuno Maru*, the *Benford* and *Busby*, who were the ships who really formed the Federation.

The glory went to the far travelers, but the dirty work went to the Destroyer-class ships, the gunboats of space, who put down revolt and international war, who delivered the mail and medicine, who guarded the cargo lanes and brought a form and substance to the Great Alliance.

Such a ship was the *Coridon Queen*, a modestly funded Federation vessel, underarmed with defensive weaponry, an aging craft coming late to warp drive after eleven years as an interplanetary cruiser. Built as a commercial interplanetary ship, the *Lodestar IX*, by Lockheed Spaceframes, Inc., it was drafted during the African crisis of 2254, renamed the *Spacebird*, and used on the Earth-Mars run until 2261, when it was transferred to the Federation Star Fleet and renamed—again—as the *Coridon Queen*, christened by the Coridan Ambassador to Terra.

Among those young officers and men who served aboard and went on to greater glory were Montgomery Scott (of the *Enterprise*); Tom Nellis, the writer; Elizabeth Crawley, later the Psychmorph of Crandall III; and Lyman Epstein, who was to figure later in the Bullion Caper.

Take Scott, then a young and ambitious officer, hoping for a berth in a big ship. A hard drinker and harder worker, he cut a swath with the human females in all the ports along the Eighth Sector line. In this he did not differ much from other Chief Engineers, with little hint of the glory that was to come.

On Gamma Theta IX, for instance, he met for the first time a Thorian and—foolishly, as it turned out—challenged him to a drinking bout. What the Scotsman did not know was that alcoholic beverage was like food to a Thorian: they got fat instead of drunk. The resulting bout cost Scott a month's pay and a reprimand from his captain.

But the young officer was soon to be tested far beyond what he had known. The *Coridan Queen* went to New Bavaria, third planet of Omicron Gamma, where a revolt, believed to be instigated by Klingon agents, was underway.

In orbit, Scott volunteered to go planetside as he spoke a little German, the Universal Translator being in test mode at that time. In civilian clothes he infiltrated a group of revolutionaries, this time by successfully drinking the rebel leader under the table, only to discover that there was no Klingon intervention at all, but a magnificently corrupt continental government. Upon his recommendation, the Federation removed the governor and forty-one members of his government, new elections were held, and the gross national product increased by 21 percent.

It was through these measures—not always the phaser-wielding, door-smashing heroics of the cinema—that the Federation achieved extensive peace throughout its early years.

Letter, Lt. Commander Scott to Fleet Commodore Kenneth MacAlpine, dated 23 June 2165:

Sir:

I cannot properly express my delight at the promotion you have so generously championed. I hope and trust that your faith will not be misplaced. While I found my time aboard the *Steven Barnes* interesting—especially in the Tau Ceti region, with you commanding—I look forward to my assignment aboard the U.S.S. *Enterprise* with the greatest possible eagerness.

In its short career the *Enterprise*, under its first captain, Commodore Robert April, then under Captain Christopher Pike, has made notable achievement a routine measure. I have not previous met its present captain, James Kirk, but from your description he sounds like a bonnie officer.

I was proud to serve under you, sir, and thank you again for your recommendation.

If I am ever in the vicinity of Alpha Gammelion I shall indeed come visit you, as you suggested, and tell you "tales of wonder." My best to you and your wife, the lovely Adrionne, and my wishes that your retirement be the justified rest due a fine career.

Excerpt, Ship's Log, U.S.S. Enterprise, dated 1499.0:

Table of Organization
Commanding Officer: Captain Christopher Pike
First Officer: Lieutenant Commander Leigh Hudec
Science Officer: Lieutenant Commander Spock
Medical Officer: Dr. Paul Piper (relieving Dr. Joseph Boyce as of this date.)
Navigator: José Tyler
Senior Geologist: Lieutenant Arthur D'Amato
Communications Officer: Lieutenant Shirley Goldstein
Chief Engineering Officer: Lieutenant Commander Clegg Pitcairn

Excerpt, Ship's Log, U.S.S. Enterprise, dated 1513.7:

Table of Organization
Commanding Officer: Captain James T. Kirk
First Officer/Science Officer: Lieutenant Commander Spock
Medical Officer: Dr. Leonard McCoy
Chief Engineering Officer: Lieutenant Commander Montgomery Scott
Communications Officer: Lieutenant Nyota Uhura
Navigator: Lieutenant Hikaru Sulu

Senior Geologist: Lieutenant Arthur D'Amato
A-and-A Officer: Lieutenant Carolyn Palamas

**Letter, Lt. Vincent DeSalle, Assistant Chief Engineer, to Linda
Feng Kuo-chang, dated 29 May 2167:**

Just my standard write-every-night-and-mail-in-sometime port letter. I told you yesterday about Chief Scott, about how he fixed the antimatter pod when none of us even knew that something was wrong. "You get a feeling, laddie," he said to me then.

Today I asked again, "How did he know?" (I mean, it could have popped and we'd be component atoms looking for a places to dust down on—!) What he said was this:

"Learn the engines, laddie, learn them so you know their song in your sleep. The slightest thing and you'll come right up out of a dream with yourself and your lassie on some Coridan beach"—I've mentioned you to him and shown him those pictures we took in the Seychelles—"you'll breathe with them, you'll feel them around you, and when they're sick, you'll know."

I know that sounds, well, almost crazy, but it *works!* He really can tell, almost like they were speaking to him! I'm an engineer and I think a good one, though Jimmy Gabler is better, but Mr. Scott is *so* much better that, well, there's no comparison.

I hope I never get transferred out of here until I'm at least half as good as Mr. Scott.

All my love. I know five years seems like a long time, but there's only four more to go. Give Ching my love.

Excerpt, letter from Lt. Charlene Masters to Randolph Masters, dated 1704.6:

. . . But the big news is Lt. Riley. Well, we came to PSI 2000 to pick up a research party because this planet was ready to go pop, but they were all dead. Mr. Spock and Joe Tormolen (I told you about him, he's the depressed one) seemed to have gotten some wild virus that relaxes inhibitions and brings out one's basic nature. (I better not get infected again or this ship is *not* safe!)

Joe tried to take his own life, but Lt. Sulu (he's the cute nav officer) and Kevin Riley (he's the one that thinks being Irish is an excuse for anything) got infected, too, in trying to stop Joe.

It was a water-borne virus, carried in perspiration and spread by touch, and we all got it! Luckily, I don't remember much, and we're catching up on each other by running ship's tapes when we have a chance. Lieutenant Sulu started running around like some kind of old-time hero waving a fencing foil. I saw the chief nurse, Miss Chapel, who got it early, acting positvely *sexy!*

Kevin Riley, though, really got us in deep trouble. He locked himself in the engine room, cut out all the auxiliaries, and had Mr. Scott in a real flying tizzy. This PSI 2000's got gravity that fluctuates—one of the reasons it's going pop, probably to reform and start over in a few thou years. But it got us yanked out of orbit. The Great Floppero if something wasn't done, and that numbskull Riley was locked in!

I heard Captain Kirk got all mooney and romantic and that Mr. Spock—MISTER SPOCK!—was seen crying about his mother and how she had suffered on Vulcan. Dr. McCoy came through as usual, but down here, Riley was singing "I'll Take You Home Again, Kathleen" over the speakers and we couldn't get to him to detox the nut.

It was really close—I mean, *close*. But Mr. Scott and Mr. Spock really came through. They were pretty unorthodox about it—I'll spare you the scientific details as I know you don't understand (just as you don't understand how & why your one and only daughter loves planet-hopping). But Mr. Scott is a bona fide hero around here, let me tell you!

Excerpt, The Gods of Space, by Walter Ackerman:

One of the best-documented account of true gods—as opposed to highly intelligent beings—is in the log of the famed starship *Enterprise*.

Locally it was 3468.1, near Pollux IV. Some sort of force drew the ship there, and they met a being, humanlike in every aspect, who claimed to be Apollo, last of the ancient Greek gods. The others, he claimed, had died of loneliness since departure from Mount Olympus. My personal feeling is that they died for a lack of faith, their powers weakening as humans ceased to believe in them.

Sensors revealed that this creature had superhuman, perhaps even supernatural, characteristics derived from an organic ability to use energy from sources outside himself. He manifested storms, thunderbolts, and other phenomena, then transformed himself into a giant.

All attempts by Captain James T. Kirk and his men to escape were hampered by one of their own crewmen: Lieutenant Carolyn Palamas, whom Apollo wanted for his bride.

It is to be noted that supplementary sources reveal that Lieutenant Commander Montgomery Scott, Chief Engineering Officer, had other plans for the young officer. He was not displeased, sources say, when Captain Kirk impressed the female officer with the need to reject the advances of the god Apollo.

Members of the crew located the power source of the god and destroyed it, whereupon Apollo, undoubtedly in the terminal phase of self-destruction already, spread himself thinly upon the wind and disappeared, to paraphase the record.

Lieutenant Commander Scott did not pursue the case further; it must be difficult to try to follow a god.

Letter, Lieutenant Commander Montgomery Scott to Lieutenant Commander Mikhail Manescu, dated 6 November 2167:

I know that, as a former Chief Engineer on the *Constellation*, you are as saddened as I that the great old ship has been destroyed. But I want you to know she went bravely; her last act was one we can all honor.

I'm certain you must have read the official as well as the popular accounts, but just in case you were still out there in the Coalsack with the *Yorktown* when this all happened, I'll give you a brief idea of the circumstances of her death.

There was this great ship—we called it the

Doomsday Machine—that wandered into our galaxy from God knows where. It had been eating its way along the Perseus arm for eons, I guess. It was a robot ship as much as we can discern, which could break up planets and eat them, as it were, for fuel. As a result, it had the tendency to go right through the most populated areas, like any Scot through Free Drink time.

Commodore Matthew Decker—you remember him from the *Exeter*, I believe—was commanding and brought the *Connie* smack up against her, trying to blast the beastie. But it didn't work that way, and we found the good ship crippled, the crew killed to the last man, and Decker in poor shape.

Captain Kirk—you must remember him, I introduced you in San Francisco that time you and I and those two Centauri blondes on leave from that Jupiter-run ship, the *Red Planet* or the *Ceres*, one or the other—anyway, the Captain beamed Decker aboard, and I got sent over to see if I could get the *Constellation* to run.

You've never seen such a mess, Mike. The antimatter pods were deframed, ready to blow at any moment. Power down to a trickle from the batteries. The Cochrane warp drive totally gone, not even the main generator in its cradle. The thrusters collapsed, the M-6 and the XR-17 blown. The impulse engines were down, the J-7s burnt out from 5 to 8, and the whole place burning, smoky, as real a mess as ye could find.

I rewired the J-7 around to 9 & 10, hooked in 1-4 through the transverser unit, blocked the servos, and set the transmuter at minus 5. Yes, a living bomb, as it were.

At the last minute we transported back, flew the *Constellation* right into the maw of that thing—you cannot believe the size! The ship was like a fly going down the throat of some singer at an outdoor night show!

We blew her inside. The matter-antimatter implosion just fragmented that berserker. It was a bonnie ship, but it went down in a good cause. You have reason to be proud, for she hung together right until the last, and I tell you, she was hurting badly.

So that's the story, the way it really happened.

Your friend, Montgomery Scott

Subspace message, full text, Commander Montgomery Scott to Sarek and Amanda, Vulcan; dated 7 Aug 2183:

My condolences upon the death of your son. He was not only one of the finest officers I ever had the privilege of serving with, but he was my friend. You have every reason to be proud of him, and if there is any consolation in this, it is that he died during the enactment of a sober and logical decision that saved the ship and crew from certain death.

He shall ever remain in my heart and in the hearts of all those who knew him. I loved the man.

Spock*

SERIAL NUMBER: WR39-733-906

*Name is rendered in Universal English from the original Vulcan
according to Starfleet Directive 9-33-TL2-19, and is an accepted approximation.

PRESENT RANK: Captain
BORN: Shi Kahr, Vulcan, 56 Tasmeen 503
FATHER: Sarek
MOTHER: Amanda Grayson *(Homo sapien)*
SIBLINGS: None
MARITAL STATUS: Unmarried
CHILDREN: None
EDUCATION: Vulcan Primary School; Vulcan Academy of Sciences, University of Makropyrios; Starfleet Academy, Class 85.
STARFLEET ACADEMY GRADE AVERAGE: 4
PRIMARY LANGUAGE: Vulcan and Universal English; also Rigellian, Andorian, Coridan alpha, Trexlor, French, Creon, Baroni, Sarcaniflex, Do-an-muli.

COMMENDATIONS:
Vega Award of Merit, Comet Class
Plixar, Hydrogen Class
Z-Mangre Prize, 10th Class
King Axnar's Iridium Star
Martian Colonies Award of Merit
Federation Academy of Sciences Einstein Award
Starfleet Unit Citation, with Four Clusters
Starfleet Commendations, 97

AWARDS OF VALOR:
Denebian Star of Heroism, First Class
Axanar Medal with Nova
Coridan Order of Heroism
Procyon Order of St. Mark
Starfleet Citation for Conspicuous Gallantry
Order of the Knights of Trexlor
Federation Exceptional Service Medal
United Federation of Planets Golden Sun
Star of Sirius (Posthumous)
United Federation of Planets Golden Medal of Honor (Posthumous)

CONDEMNATIONS: None

STARFLEET ACADEMY DEMERITS: None

INTERESTS: Meditation; Terran poetry; music; 3-D chess; Trexlor *barra*

STARFLEET ASSIGNMENTS:

> U.S.S. *Sirius*, NCC-1744 (Heavy Cruiser), Assistant Science Officer
>
> U.S.S. *Phardos*, NCC-1757 (Heavy Cruiser), Science Officer
>
> U.S.S. *Enterprise*, NCC-1701 (Heavy Cruiser), Science Officer and First Officer
>
> Leave of Absence
>
> U.S.S. *Enterprise*, NCC-1701 (Heavy Cruiser), Science Officer and First Officer
>
> Starfleet Academy, staff
>
> U.S.S. *Enterprise*, NCC-1701 (Heavy Cruiser), Commanding Officer (Special circumstances)

Excerpt, letter from Cadet Spock to his mother, on Starliner Sa'ark stationery, in Universal-English, dated approximately 18 July 2142:

Greetings:

I realize that my father, your husband, does not approve of my decision to leave the Vulcan Academy of Sciences to join the Federation Starfleet. I hope that someday he will see the logic of my action.

To exercise the mind is the greatest of all actions, but to do so in the vacuum of what humans call an "ivory tower" is to stride on a treadmill. I felt I must generate new situations, to find new imput, to "exercise" in the arena of actual events.

That my father, Sarek, has refused to speak to me is unfortunate, for it denies us both participation in the mind of the other, an activity which would have been greatly to my benefit.

But Starfleet offers the greatest chance for expansion of experience I have so far found. While the Klingon race and the Romulans are closer to us in a genetic sense, it is the race called human which is the closest to us in the mental sense. While it is true that they are rigorously emotional, at times to the point of irrational behavior, they are a vigorous race, inventive, imaginative, and daring.

I do not say these things because of your human ancestry, my mother, nor because of my own hybrid state, but because it is demonstrably true.

We land at Starfleet Academy within five Terran ship days, and I shall mail this at that time. Live long and prosper.

Excerpt, letter from Cadet Spock to his mother, undated, on Starfleet Academy stationery:

Greetings. I have been informed by the Cadet Captain that it is Standard Operating Procedure for cadets to inform the parent or parents of their activities during Starfleet Academy Year One.

I find the weather here difficult, for they maintain a mean temperature here suitable for *Homo sapiens* and allied races; it is thus quite cold for Vulcans. I am, by the way, the only Vulcan attending, so it would be illogical for them to attempt a mean temperature if they included this cadet in their calculations. I wear the usual off-planet heating suit and have been given solitary quarters and permission to raise the ambient temperature there to Vulcan mean.

My fellow cadets are about what I expected from my non-Vulcan encounters. The classes are not too difficult, and I have sufficient time to meditate on what the Earthlings here call our way: Infinite Diversity in Infinite Combinations.

I have ceased to play chess, either traditional or dimensional, with any of my classmates, as they offer no opposition worth the time. Their illogical moves border on the irrational. I have played occasionally with two or three of the faculty, but they are only marginally better. The Academy computer offers an exceptional game which has the advantage of being available at any hour without any attendant conversation, and without any wounding of that useless and even dangerous appendage, the human ego.

Inform T'Pring that I am well and will return to Vulcan on commencement leave in three Terran years.

Live long and prosper.

Excerpt, Earth Through Vulcan Eyes, by Tom Nellis:

Spock, at Starfleet Academy, was singular. This is not surprising, in that Vulcans were a rarity in Starfleet in his time. But in the words of a classmate, B. J. O'Katwin, "He was a loner. He was a loner in a crowd and in class."

Another classmate, Louis Gray (later Admiral, retired) said of Spock in his autobiography, *My Years Off Earth:* "They hazed him considerably that first year, and some the second. I suppose it never stopped completely, but since he didn't react, the fun went out of it."

Excerpt, Mist/Fireflies/Stars/Us, by Lawrence van Cott:

Spock the Vulcan was an anomaly among the garrulous, fun-loving young men, women, and assorted aliens at Starfleet Academy those years. He neither drank, played pranks, ragged his teachers (except possibly in occasionally knowing more than they did about their subject), nor indulged in any of the other excesses common to youth.

Spock the Vulcan was never allowed to forget he was an alien among humans, but I don't think that was what truly set him apart. He found so few who were his equal at anything—at least at anything he considered worthwhile—that their derision, envy, and sometimes even hatred did not bother him. The distant barking of dogs to an armored man.

Spock the Vulcan was a loner, had been a loner, and remained a loner throughout his life, with the smallest circle of true friends I think any major figure in history has had. His small circle was of the highest quality, but it was, in the end and always, the smallest of circles.

Letter, T'Pau to Spock, dated 41 Kareel 540:

Note: This translation from the Vulcan text is by Richard Dorf Butner-Estrada, who says these are only approximations in Universal-English for many Vulcan terms and phrases.

Greetings:

You who are of a hybrid lineage[1] must have a difficult [untranslatable: something like time, duration, endurance, life] in the service of the human

---

1. Spock is half Vulcan, half of Terran stock.

Starfleet, for your natural reactions must be mixed. You must always remember that you must live by the Vulcan [philosophy] of no war, no crime; by order, logic and control, and not by the mind-destroying raw emotions and instincts of your human ancestry.

Your [service, duty, optional choice] with the Federation must bring you into constant and frequent opposition to Vulcan [philosophy] and tradition. While we do not condone the meaningful death of any being, we are aware that, logically, death is always with us and that the greater number can benefit from the efforts and even death of the minor number.

I saw T'Pring at the Midsummer Soltice. She was with her father and Stonn. She had with her the latest work of T'lek and Pre'al, though she did not seem to understand the principles stated therein, that of *koon-ut-kal-if-fee*.[2]

Your mother is well but she was away all summer. Terrans do not fare well during the summers here. She went to the Northern Encampment, where I was told a *Le-matya*[3] came close.

Live long and prosper.

Excerpt, Five-Year Missions, by Mulai Yusef and Joseph Heineman:

It required a certain kind of person to boldly go into the unknown. Earth had bred generations of

2. "Marriage" or "challenge." Vulcans look upon both terms as approximately equal.

3. A creature similar to a Terran mountain lion with odd, diamondlike markings and poisonous teeth; rare but not extinct Vulcan predator.

them—the Marco Polos, the Christoforo Colum-
buses, the *conquistadores* and Vikings, the immigrants who crossed the great plains of the New
World, the Armstrongs and Ballards and Grennells
who left Earth in such primitive spaceships that we
marvel at them today.

The officers and crew of a warp-drive starship
were much like those who set sail with Drake or
Magellan, far from home and long way from friendly
shores. But the dangers as well as surprises were far
more deadly, far more varied than any faced by
Captain Cook, the American mountain men, or those
who plumbed the depths of the sea.

Nor were humans the only ones in space. Space-
faring races are common, but perhaps more than
any, the human race fared farther and in more
directions from their home star. They were called
"restless" by some, "invaders" by others, "heroic"
by many.

It is a curious fact that the logical and meditative
Vulcans were among those who chose to stand by
the *Homo sapiens* on the bridges of far-reaching
starships. Dr. James Gregory, in his classic book
From Different Seas: Evolution of the Vulcan Race,
strikes a parallel between the Irish and the Vulcans,
in that many Irish fought for the English in their
wars—and, at home, fought against them. They ex-
plored with the English and yet were so different.

Yet, as Dr. Gregory and his staff at Benford University pointed out, Vulcans were considerably more
different from humans than the Irish were from the
English.

Perhaps the most prominent among all Vulcans is

Spock, the Science Officer and later Captain of the U.S.S. *Enterprise* during the most critical phase of interstellar exploration. Not the first nor the last of his race to serve with the Federation, he is certainly the most prominent.

Excerpt, Vulcan Longevity, by Jean Culbertson:

In comparing Vulcan to Earth we must understand that it has a mean temperature of 140 degrees Centigrade, a 24.98 hour day, and a 408.04-day year. The Vulcans have divided their year into quarters: Kareel, Matara, Belaar, and Tasmeen, corresponding to Winter, Spring, Summer, and Autumn.

Although the Vulcan civilization is over 9,000 years old, they date modern times from the coronation of the last Vulcan king, Sukir, who was also the first of the modern elected leaders and who brought Vulcan into the Age of Logic. The Terran year of 2100, for example, would correspond to the Vulcan calendar year of 519.

Excerpt, Starwarp; The Autobiography of Edward Leslie; Commander, Retired:

Once, on leave, I ran into a senior officer who had been in the same class at the Academy with Mr. Spock. She told me: "He was always polite, but distant, even as a young man. Of course, Vulcans live so much longer that I guess he wasn't such a young man at that, having spent a very long time at the Vulcan Academy of Sciences."

She went on to say that he created an aura of

mystery around him—quite unconsciously, she in-
sisted—that made the females at the Academy, and
perhaps even some of the faculty, more than ordi-
narily interested. "But as far as I know, he never had
anything to do with them. His idea of a big night
was to get a Draw out of the computer at chess."

Once, she said, they were in the recreational dis-
trict and saw Mr. Spock walking about. "We
couldn't believe it! We tracked him all through the
arcades, the sleazos, the simulators, and kept trying
to figure out what or who he was after. The only time
he paused at all was passing a simulator booth. It
was Praxis-13, which was new then and driving us
all crazy trying to win. He watched some cadet fub
it, then stepped in and in twenty seconds had hit a
million points and quit. A million points! Jardine
was our best computer gamester then and the highest he got on the Praxis was 450,000, and that only
once!"

She said they followed the Vulcan cadet farther
and into the oldest part of the Academy station.
"You could see the old-type welds, even bolts and
rivets! And there we found what he had been looking
for! It was a dim room with a few lights and a lot of
very illegal smoking of tobacco. Really creepy, like
an old movie.

"Along the wall was this old man, really ancient
he seemed to us, and before him was a Commodore!
They were playing chess, and the old man was
winning! Here and there around the room were a lot
of people—I recognized a retired Admiral, two of the
Senior Staff, three Andorians, and several others of
different ages and sexes.

"Spock waited, and we waited, back in the shadows. I fell asleep until Etienne de Ville put an elbow in my ribs. Spock was playing . . . and winning! You could cut the tension in the room with a knife! People were sweating, money was being wagered, and everyone was asking who the cadet was!

"Spock lost, but just barely, I understand, and word was the next time he went down, he beat the old man. No, Spock was a singular individual. If he was a human, I'd say he was superhuman. But he's a Vulcan."

Ship's Log, U.S.S. Sirius, NCC-1744, Captain Gregory Calkins, Commanding, Stardate 998.8:

Patrolling this date in the Procyon-Alpha sector we received a signal from an MK-IV Starliner, the *Queen of Vega-Prime*, indicating they were under attack from a Klingon vessel of the Belsar class.

Approaching at Warp 4, we decelerated and emerged from warp space 1.3 parsecs from the Procyon-Alpha Epislon system. We were almost immediately fired upon by the Klingon vessel. As per standard Starfleet Operations Directive 45-73-A, we emerged into normal space with shields up and thus avoided damage.

However, the Klingon vessel refused to disengage from its attack upon the unarmed tourist ship, and we had to open fire to save lives. An extended engagement ensued in which our starboard deflector shields were overloaded by repeated photon torpedo strikes.

Lieutenant Spock, my Assistant Science Officer on

duty in the Fire Control Center, used the brief moment of downed shields to fire out ten conventional-atomic torpedos with self-directing controllers keyed to Klingon warp-drive emissions. That Mr. Spock had the foresight to prepare the torpedos and to eject them at the time when they might be mistaken for debris from the strike is exceptional.

With timed-delay activators, the torpedos drifted out of the immediate battle area, then struck when the Klingon vessel was otherwise engaged. The stern shields were downed, then the port shields, and we disabled the ship at once.

The Klingon vessel was immobilized and is under tow at this moment, back to Starbase 9 for interment and trial of captain and officers.

The successful outcome of the engagement was due primarily to Lieutenant Spock's quick thinking.

I recommend to Starfleet Command that he be awarded the appropriate award for valor.

Chapter Ten, Spock, The Human Vulcan, by Lisa Araminta:

Spock was a Senior Lieutenant when transferred to the U.S.S. *Phardos* during routine maintenance at Starbase 10. He performed his new duties as Senior Science Officer well, despite considerable bias from Captain Abd-ul-Aziz. The commanding officer, veteran of seven years as a starship commander and the Battle of Meritormallion against a Klingon force, persisted in insulting and degrading the Vulcan officer at every opportunity.

Lieutenant Spock voiced no protest despite urgings from the other officers that the captain was

exerting unusual pressure and exhibiting "scandal-
ous" prejudice. "Pointed-eared devil" and "Vulcan
Satan" were his two most commonly used phrases.

Evidently Spock decided that he could not effi-
ciently or effectively continue his duties as Science
Officer and put in a request for transfer at earliest
convenient date. The captain refused approval and
doubled his attacks upon the Vulcan, questioning
his scientific advice, ridiculing his appearance, issu-
ing reprimands and demerits at every opportunity
until his irrational behavior grew so horrendous
that he had antagonized all but one of the other
officers.

This situation was complicated by the ship's arrival at Mezieres Alpha IV, a medium-sized water
world, Class III. Captain Abd-ul-Aziz ordered Spock
to transport down with a trio of security men and an
A-and-A officer, Lieutenant Tania Bogolyubski. Pre-
liminary survey orbit had located some sort of life-
form readings on or beneath the surface of this blue
planet.

Donning protective suits, the party undertook one
of the most dangerous of transporter trips, that
which materializes the subject beneath a liquid.
There is always the danger of insufficient spacial
thrust—which while working well in many types of
gaseous substances, works less well in liquid—and
that a portion of that liquid will be left within the
materialized subject.

But the transfer was of an excellent nature, and
they found themselves in a kind of underwater
dome, an undulating rocky material that Spock's
tricorder stated was a type of coral.

The structure was obviously designed, though not necessarily by human or humanoid minds, and extended for a kilometer or two in every direction. It was a vast honeycombed building with entrance and exits on all six sides of an enclosure, a design only possible in a liquid medium or a null-gravity zone.

Up from the surrounding opening came a group of seallike creatures—though far from the sleek Aquans, or Argo, that Spock was to meet quite some years later. These were not at all humanoid, and their fins were incapable of using any but the most primitive tools. Nevertheless, they were quite intelligent, and the *Phardos* crewmen did not attempt either escape or attack while they were examined.

Then suddenly, without warning, the very floor beneath them heaved and surged, and walls sprang up around them in seconds. The walls seemed to *form*, to grow, speck by speck, as if accreting directly out of the seawater around them.

"Do not panic," Spock advised over the intrasuit radio. He examined the tubelike structure as it built its way up over them, holding out the tricorder. One of the security men, however, grew too frightened and attempted to swim upward, out of the tube, but it closed in around him even faster, capturing and holding his leg. The security man drew his phaser and was about to fire when Lieutenant Spock, using his own phaser, disintegrated a section of the wall and ordered the others outside.

The panicking security man blasted away at the rocklike substance imprisoning his foot, and brought down the tower in a flickering crash of disintegrating particles that would have injured or destroyed Spock, Bogolyubski, and the other security men.

The seallike Meziereans were astounded, yet rallied quickly enough to cause another tube of rocklike material to form around them. This time Spock used his phaser without hesitation, destroying the imprisoning material at once.

Spock then attempted communication by standard means, but was unsuccessful. The Meziereans then attacked, using only their teeth, but the protective suits were too tough. Lieutenant Spock then grappled with an attacker and held him tightly while he used the Vulcan mind meld for a long, agonizing moment.

Spock then released the native life form and announced to his landing party the news that the Meziereans were harmless. "They control a kind of coral creature, which is almost microscopic and swims in the entire sea in the trillions, by telepathy. These coral analogs form buildings, walls, traps, tools, cages, and anything else needed. They link surface molecules and die, becoming stiff and rock like in fractions of a second.

"We were intruders," Spock told them, "and we had to be trapped and examined. But now all is well."

They finished the anthropological survey quickly and returned to the ship before the air supply ran out. But the captain refused to accept Lieutenant Spock's report, saying that the famous Vulcan mind meld was a trick and a fraud and that he, Spock, was in league with an alien species to destroy the *Phardos* and the Federation.

Faced with this display of totally irrational behavior, Spock did the only logical thing. He asked the ship's doctor, Ashikaga Kiyomori, to examine the captain. The reported response was, "Are you kidding? He's as loony as a Vegan circle-bird."

The doctor explained in more precise language that latent xenophobic tendencies had surfaced ever since Spock had come aboard. "It's all right to know about Vulcans, even to know there are some in Starfleet, but to have one right under your aristocratic nose—!"

Invoking the proper section of the regulations dealing with an incapacitated commanding office, Lieutenant Spock put Captain Abd-ul-Aziz in a medical stasis, reported to Starfleet Command, and was ordered home.

At the ensuing court-martial Lieutenant Spock was exonerated and received another Starfleet commendation. But he was also transferred to the *Enterprise*, Captain Christopher Pike commanding.

Letter, Christopher Pike to his brother, Holden Pike, Stardate 1001.6:

Dear Holden:

I hope you and Virginia are doing well there on that iridium rock of yours. It's hard to believe that after two hundred years of space travel no one noticed a chunk of almost pure iridium bumping around in the asteriod belt. You'll be rich and can support an old starship captain on half-pay when I retire!

Hope little Chris has learned that in space you can make a mistake *once*. You don't get a second chance, usually. Living in a pressure pod on the side of a tumbling piece of metal a kilometer long must make the stars look like a bright set of ferris wheels.

I'm doing as well as can be expected. Had a narrow escape on a place called Talos IV, but I can't tell you any more; they are quarantining it as of 1001.8.

I've got a fantastic ship here. The best! My Number One is Lieutenant Commander Leigh Hudec, a formidable woman of considerable experience. She commanded the *Bowie*, a scout ship, during a fleet engagement with the Klingons, and the *Suleiman*—that's a destroyer-class ship that's a dandy—during a Romulan violation of the Treaty Zone. She was Number One on the cruiser *K'Hotan*, so I'm lucky to get her. (She probably ought to be commanding her own heavy cruiser, but there are always dinosaurs among the high command.)

My science officer is a Vulcan. Took a bit of getting used to, I must say. I'd hardly ever even *met* a Vulcan before—there are sadly few of them in Starfleet—so I suppose I had a lot of those standard prejudices and dumb ideas about them. I must admit that for the first weeks, while we were testing out the updating on the ship and on the way out to Sector Eight, I'd look over to my right and see that pointed-eared Vulcan sitting there and I'd kind of jump inside!

But after a while if I looked over and he wasn't there, or someone else had relieved him, I thought it was wrong. Wherever I go, up, down, or sideways in this fleet, I'd like to have him there at my side. First-rate officer. Can't say he's a barrel of laughs, but then I'm pretty sober-sided, too, I guess.

The ship's doctor is Paul Piper—you may remember him from when you visited me on board the *Betelguese*. We're losing him, though. He says he's getting too old to be planet-hopping.

My Chief Nav is José Tyler, who I had on the *Darius*, that great old destroyer. (Is it true they scrapped her?) My chief engineering officer is Clegg Pitcairn. Virginia, you may remember him from my graduation ceremony at the Academy—he was the cadet who stepped on your foot so gracefully he gave Holden green pangs.

Well, they tell me I must go be a commanding officer type now, so I'll finish this off and have it subspaced on computer interface, so you should get it soon, if your rock hasn't collided with another one. Yes, I know, they say they have every single one tagged with a transponder and that you could fly a dreadnought through there blindfolded, just letting the computer mind the rocks for you, but there's always one they missed!

Love, Chris

Excerpt, The Voyages of the U.S.S. Enterprise, by John Griffin:

The story of Captain Christopher Pike has been told many times and many ways, but perhaps the best and clearest record appears in the court-martial record of Lieutenant Commander Spock, the Vulcan science officer who served under both Pike and, later, James T. Kirk.

According to testimony, Captain Pike was horribly scarred and disfigured beyond the aid of any cosmetic surgeon during an accidental radiation incident. Spock, serving under Kirk (Stardate 3012.4), found the crippled and nearly inarticulate Pike on Starbase 11, and was quite shaken by the meeting and by the appearance of his former commanding officer.

Lieutenant Commander Spock, by misdirecting and tampering with an entire complex of ship's computers, took over the *Enterprise* completely. He locked the autopilot in such a way it could not be reset, then turned himself in to Captain James Kirk for trial, as the ship headed for Talos IV, a planet— the *only* planet—placed off limits by General Order Number 7.

Violation of that order is punishable by death.

During the trial, which took place on the *Enterprise* as it headed toward Talos IV, via subspace communication with Starfleet Command, the rest of the story was revealed.

Some years before, during Pike's command of the brand-new *Enterprise*, fresh from the San Francisco Navy Yard, Captain Pike had been captured during a routine survey by small, cerebral, subterranean Talosians. He was to serve as breeding stock for a hardier race that could live on the harsh surface of Talos IV.

The Talosians had used illusion generation for such an extended period of time that it had weakened them as a race. They needed strong pioneers. The Talosians used a human girl, Vina, the survivor of an earlier ship crash on Talos, to capture Pike's interest. Vina was presented to Pike in the form of a Rigellian female in distress, then a warm and loving Earth girl, then a very sexual Orion slave dancer.

But Pike would not cooperate with his captor's plans to have him mate.

The Talosians then brought down other females from the starship, using their powers of illusion. But Captain Pike threatened to kill all of them unless they were released, and the Talosians decided that human beings were much too violent to be useful and too individual to be easily controlled. The *Enterprise* people were set free, but Vina decided to remain on Talos. Without the Talosian illusions she was ugly and deformed from her crash injuries, and she decided that remaining was best.

During the court-martial, the Talosians appeared themselves, utilizing the ship's videoscreens, admitting that their powers extended somewhat farther than Starfleet had anticipated. The Talosians offered to let Captain Pike live out his life with them, giving him once again the feeling of being young, healthy, and uncrippled.

Starfleet permitted this and, in view of Lieutenant Commander Spock's exemplary record, dropped all charges.

It is believed that Captain Pike still lives on Talos, young and healthy, in the company of the beautiful young Earth girl, Vina: two illusions everyone thought beautiful.

Excerpt, postscript to official message, Admiral Jay Mallory to Captain James T. Kirk, aboard the U.S.S. Enterprise, dated 1 Aug 2166:

Dear Jim:

I'd like to add my personal congratulations as well as my official ones to your new command. They couldn't have picked a finer officer. The *Enterprise* is a special ship, and you have as your Number One an unusual officer in Lieutenant Commander Spock.

I know you'll have read his dossier, but I thought I'd add some personal notes—everything, as you well know, does not show up in the official files. (Darned good thing, too! I can think of at least a dozen incidents I'm glad are not in my file!)

Spock's an unusual officer. He's half-human, you know. Mother was a teacher who went to Vulcan—though how she takes that inhumanly hot place I'll never understand. She married Ambassador Sarek, the finest Vulcan I ever knew. (Takes Benjisidriac for heart attacks, you know.)

Spock, like all Vulcans, is naturally immune to Saurian viris, auroral plague, and Pelzarian bloodworms. Better have your medical officer stock up on info and anything special he thinks might be needed. You're going out for a long trip and Starfleet Medical Center will not be down the block.

He inherited one of those I-Chayas from his father. Those tricky little pets are immensely long-lived, longer than Vulcans even, and are *most* unusual. (Read up on them.) Anyone who can make a pet of one of *those* things is rare, to say the least.

He's quite accomplished, you know. His chess rating is Computer-Equal, so don't try to razzle-dazzle him with your play, and *forget* trying to psyche him out the way you did me at Lunabase. He's a whiz at the computer deck, so rely on him for that. He's a Class III in the handling of the Ahn-wuon, that oldest of Vulcan weapons, as well as the lirpa. Not a bad phaser shot, either.

How do I know all this? Well, for one thing, he was

Science Officer for Chris Pike, and before that I had him at Starfleet Academy. The most serious student you ever saw, too, bar none. And the smartest. Diplomatic, too; he caught me in an error on some math and very gently led me around so that I could correct myself without looking like a fool before the students.

He studied under Sakar at the Vulcan Academy of Sciences and was second in the class, so you are not getting a bonehead, Jim.

I hate to put down some personal things, but often those are the truly revealing things. A commander *should* know everything, of course, about his ship *and* his crew. I mean *everything*. Then he or she should learn to selectively ignore. (For example, I am well aware who "appropriated" the liter of Saurian brandy I had cached in my quarters at the Academy, but I figured the "appropriator" deserved it after outfoxing the simulator. And I *had* said "Get yourself a drink.") All leaders should learn how to ignore. You already know not to give an order that cannot or will not be obeyed, but one of those little things they never *quite* say at SFA is Learn to Look the Other Way.

But unless you know everything, you can't know what to ignore. So: Spock was betrothed to a Vulcan female called T'Pring at or near birth. That's the way they do things on Vulcan, and who knows if that's right or wrong.

You have a loyal officer in Spock. If you earn his loyalty you'll never lose it, and I think that loyalty will be one of the greatest pleasures in your life, son.

Have a good voyage. I'll be up for retirement

about the time you get back and I have my eye on a little island in the Ionian sea. Enough of running about the galaxy. I'll leave that to the younger lads like yourself.

But before I go on the beach I am placing a bet with myself: that you'll make admiral someday soon. Since I fully plan on winning that bet, there's a favor I'd like to ask of you. (No, not a case of bootleg Saurian.) *Pass it on*. That's all. You've kept saying you owe me something for helping to get you into the Academy, so pass it on. Find some bright young person and give him or her a boost. Pass the favor *on* rather than paying it back.

As the Vulcans say, "Live long and prosper."

Excerpt, Private Diary, by Christine Chapel; dated 24 December 2168:

It is never to be?

I cannot explain my feelings, even to myself. My longings are inexpressible. His entire background, heritage, and manner defeats any attempts by me to penetrate to his heart.

But he is half human, and it is to that half I attempt to appeal. But it is like throwing yourself at a rock wall. There are times in which I think he *wants* to break out, to burst forth, to show his feelings for me. (He *must* have feelings for me!) There are times when I almost wish he might show his emotions to another woman. At least then I might be able to fight, to cope, to know that I had a chance.

But he cuts himself off from all emotion. It is that

damnable Vulcan blood! It runs green and cold in him, denying the feelings and emotions of others. No, he *acknowledges* that others have feelings, but does not understand them.

I tried appealing to him in a *logical* way, but I only confused him, for whatever I did, it seemed illogical to me.

It is hard, seeing him every watch, being near him, touching him, even on occasion caring for him. How long can I last? Am I doomed to this fruitless task of scaling a sheer rock wall with no footholds? I must be mad.

But I continue. I shall always continue to try.

Excerpt, The Death of Captain Spock, by Randall Lofficier:

Commander Scott recalled vividly the moment. "I knew Spock was dead. He was still standing, but the radiation had gotten to him. There was no hope. My heart sank. He had saved us all, but at the supreme sacrifice.

"Captain Kirk ran into the engine room, and Dr. McCoy and I could barely restrain him from plunging through the radiation lock. He called out, 'Spock!' But the Vulcan had slipped to the floor and lay slumped against the transparent lead glass lock. Perhaps it was an attempt to prevent anyone from entering, I don't know.

"The captain knelt, pressed himself against the plastic wall. A sickness rose up in me unlike anything I had ever felt before. Not even the death of my own nephew, Peter Preston, only a short time before, affected me so much.

"Spock's voice was weak over the intercom. He spoke with difficulty. 'Ship . . .out of danger?' The captain, 'Yes,' and his voice was ragged and harsh. Mr. Spock knew what was happening, knew the effect of his death on his old friend. 'Don't grieve, Admiral,' he said. 'It is logical.' I let out a cry, for this incredible person still thought as he had always thought. His sacrifice had been deliberate. 'The needs of the many,' he said with effort, '. . . outweigh . . .'

"He couldn't finish, and Captain Kirk finished it for him. '. . . the needs of the few.'

"Mr. Spock may have attempted a smile, I'm not certain. 'Or the one,' he said, clearing his throat. The captain was overcome with grief and looked away for a moment. Mr. Spock spoke again. 'I never took the . . . the Kobayashi Maru test. Until now. What do you think of . . . my solution?'

"Captain Kirk cried out, 'Spock!' as we saw the Vulcan slump. His breathing was labored and slow, his skin mottled and seared. He put his hand against the shield, his fingers spread in the Vulcan salute. 'I have been . . . and always will be . . . *your friend!*' His voice was harsh. 'Live long and prosper,' he said, and died.

"Captain Kirk cried out in protest, but it was over. We all just stared, tears running down our faces. I turned away at last and ordered a team to suit up in the heaviest of radiation armor—a long and cumbersome process, too long a process for Mr. Spock to have finished in time."

Captain Spock's remains were placed in a coffin created out of a missile container. The burial ceremony took place at Torp Bay 2. Present were Captain James Kirk, Commander Montgomery Scott, Dr. McCoy, Lieutenant Commander Nyota Uhura, Lieutenant Commander Hikaru Sulu, Dr. Carol Marcus, Dr. David Marcus, Saavik, Lieutenant Commander Chekov, and several members of the launch crew and burial detail.

This is the recorded text of the eulogy by Captain James Kirk:

"We are assembled here, today, to pay final respects to our honored dead. And yet, it should be noted that, in the midst of our sorrow, this death takes place in the shadow of new life.

"The sunrise of a new world. A world that our beloved comrade gave his life to protect and nourish. He did not feel this sacrifice a vain or an empty one. And we will not debate his profound wisdom at these proceedings.

"Of my friend, I can only say this: Of all the souls I have encountered in my travels, his was the most . . . human."

Lieutenant Commander Sulu ordered the honor guard to proceed, and Commander Scott played the bagpipe. The capsule entered the launching chamber and was shot out. It came to rest on a barren planet pocketed with craters, an airless world long ago devastated by meteor storms.

And the Genesis Project started to work.

General Information Signal from Starfleet Command to all ships, bases, stations, and commands, #3-7-2182

To all Starfleet personnel:
It is with grave personal grief that I announce the

death of Captain Spock aboard the U.S.S. *Enterprise*, NCC-1701, during an encounter with the renegade known as Khan Noonian Singh. The noble and self-less sacrifice of Captain Spock which resulted in the loss of his life was above and beyond the standards expected of Starfleet officers.

Captain Spock gave his life to save his ship and all those within her. There is no greater sacrifice anyone can make.

I send the condolences of the General Staff, the Council of the United Federation of Planets, and myself to his family on Vulcan. Starfleet had no finer officer. His standards of conduct reflect greatness upon those of us who survive.

These few bleak words cannot truly express the feelings of all of us here.

(Signed) Grand Admiral Stephen Turner, commanding

General Order 65-43/A, 2182:

To all Starfleet personnel:

Starfleet Command announces the posthumous award of the United Federation of Planets Medal of Honor to Captain Spock, U.S.S. *Enterprise*, NCC-1701, for action above and beyond the call of duty.

(Signed) Grand Admiral Stephen Turner, Commanding

Sulu, Hikaru

SERIAL NUMBER: SH203-622

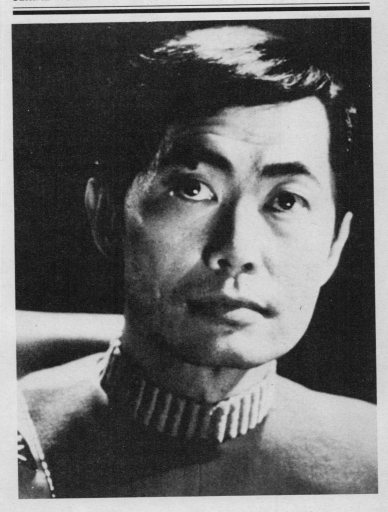

PRESENT RANK: Lieutenant Commander
BORN: Wailuku, Maui, Hawaii, Terra, 3 July 2141
FATHER: Liholiho Sulu
MOTHER: Kalea Graef Hatoyama
SIBLINGS:
>   (Hikaru Sulu)
>   Kamehameha Fujiwara Sulu
>   Liliuokalani Dani Suly
MARITAL STATUS: Unmarried
CHILDREN: None
EDUCATION: Non-standard: Mother is a consulting agronomist and the family traveled extensively at or near the frontier of human space, so Sulu received a varied education, mostly through his father, a poet. However, subject completed a year of primary school and two years of secondary school on Ganjitsu (collog.: Shinpai); Starfleet Academy Class 102
STARFLEET ACADEMY GRADE AVERAGE: 2.1
PRIMARY LANGUAGE: English, Japanese, Ganjitsuian; also Hawaiian, French, Creon, Sarcaniflex, Baroni
COMMENDATIONS:
>   Martian Colonies Award of Merit
>   Star of Trexlor
>   Starfleet Unit Citation with Two Clusters
>   Starfleet Commendations: 16
AWARDS OF VALOR:
>   Silver Palm
>   Coridan Order of Heroism
>   Procyon Order of St. Mark
>   Axanar Medal with Lightning Bolt
>   Star of Sirius
>   Starfleet Citation for Conspicuous Gallantry
>   Federation Exceptional Service Medal
CONDEMNATIONS: None
STARFLEET ACADEMY DEMERITS: 21

INTERESTS: Botony and xenobotany; firearms; fencing; biochemistry; entomology; Tarleen art; Ganjitsu fighting techniques

STARFLEET ASSIGNMENTS:

U.S.S. *Sacajawea*, NCC-598 (Scout Ship), Assistant Helmsman

U.S.S. *Crockett*, NCC-600 (Scout Ship) Helmsman

U.S.S. *Kublai*, NCC-507 (Destroyer), Helmsman

U.S.S. *Arcturus*, NCC-1807 (Heavy Cruiser), First Helmsman

U.S.S. *Enterprise*, NCC-1701 (Heavy Cruiser) Chief Helmsman

Starfleet Academy, staff

U.S.S. *Republic*, NCC-1371 (Heavy Cruiser), Chief Helmsman

U.S.S. *Krieger*, NCC-1726 (Heavy Cruiser), Chief Helmsman

U.S.S. *Enterprise*, NCC-1701 (Heavy Cruiser), Chief Helmsman

U.S.S. *Regulus*, NCC-1840 (Heavy Cruiser), Chief Helmsman

U.S.S. *Enterprise*, NCC-1701 (Heavy Cruiser), Chief Helmsman

---

Letter, Kalea Sulu to her son, dated 13 July, 2162:

Your father and I wish you well in your studies at Starfleet. But so far away! We cannot possibly visit you, so we both hope you will get to travel home at year's end.

We are proud of you here, passing those fearful tests. I know Neldin failed (and rather badly, I hear), and he was often thought quite intelligent.

I know that you believe your father is against you joining Starfleet and that you had words. But he really isn't. He's a poet and the quasi-military aspect of Starfleet grates him the wrong way. He wants only what is reasonable and practical for you—which I admit seems contrary, coming from a poet.

The sad thing, of course, is that in a sense we feel we have lost a son. In our travels the only permanent thing was *us*, the family, and those who are, or were, "family" to us. I say we have lost you to your dreams.

By now you know that Misaye will not wait, nor do I believe you thought she would. She is young, beautiful and as talented an agronomist as I. She has been offered a astonishing project on Kanter IV—designing the agronomy of an entire planet!— which will take her half her life. I have taken the liberty of advising her to find another, as much as I would like her as a daughter-in-law.

Your father just interrupted me to say that he hopes you will do well and bring honor upon the house.

And now, as to disposition of your plants here. (Your foils, weapons, music tapes and such have been put into capsule storage and welded to the exterior of the ship.) I cannot keep the feeding schedule straight with your Tellurian greencat, so I have offered him to George Temmu, who fancies it. He says he will give it back if you return, or if we cross paths. (I shamed him for that "if!"), but he says he keeps the baby plants. Your demur is doing well; it sits on the porch here at Millard with a view of the bay. I gave all your terrestrial plants to your cousin Rachel—who said to say Hi and that Marybeth remembers you, too. (I suspect that means something I should not know about!)

By season's end we shall be finished here. We have two contracts offered, one to o'Poloneo (that's in the Painters) and another to a double planet system in the Schnaubelt region. The first pays better but the other is more interesting. We'll let you know what we decide.

Goodbye for now, my son. We all love you here.

PS: You missed signing one of the family power-of-attorney papers, but Mr. Dole-Andrews says he'll send it along and you can have it notarized there.

Letter, Lieutenant Sean DePaul to Lieutenant Hikaru Sulu, dated 1508.2:

Hey, hey, hey! Ass't helmsman on a scout ship, huh, ol' buddy? They got me doing a milk run from Luna/Prime to the good moons of Jupiter. Borrowing! A lot different from Starfleet Academy, right? Oh, I'm in a Class 1 tug, dragging along a batch of transport containers every time. Boy, I wish they could develop the small ship transporter beam so we could just zap all this stuff out here.

I'm writing this letter with the gas giant in the port, a glass of white wine at my elbow, and Elayne and the Elephants on the box. But that's no sub for a *real* starship! I envy you, brudder, I really do. Hope some day we can serve together, though!

Letter, Lieutenant Hikaru Sulu to mother, dated 1510.9:

I was First Helmsman on the *Crockett*, and I'm back to being an Assistant (though a First Ass't!), but I don't mind because the *Kublai* is a destroyer and it's a real advance. There's not that much difference in the controls, just more of them, so I'm doing all right.

We orbited Gamma Lambda II a few days ago, and I got myself on my first planetfall! Of course, it's a dirty little place—a Terran colony about six years old, populated mostly by German and Dutch—in the middle of a terrible winter. Their inflated domes are half-covered in a pinkish snow. But it was *another world!*

Then we went to Sigma Chi-14, a totally different place! Warm, sunny, like the Big Island in summer. The seas are greenish, the sky is dark, and they have some kind of tree here that looks like a fat palm tree with bluish fronds. No coconuts, but something like mint apples! Other than that, Kona to four points!

The colonists there are from France and Peru mostly—quite a combination, huh? But there's a native life form, with about the IQ of a good, intelligent dog. Not big enough to be any good as labor, and not intelligent enough on the scale to count as an indigenous life form. But they wander into everything and make a mess! Good to put feet on land again, though, especially sand and surf!

On the way now to Iota Tau Psi. The only thing I know about it is that there's an intelligent life form there, NSP [Non–Space Traveling] and far from humanlike. I love it already.

Later: There's a mountain here that reminds me of

Haleakala, a volcano with great sloping sides covered with a yellow, red, and green jungle! The locals are called Berefords, after the Earthman who typed them for the UFP. They're tall and stately, but can move as quick and as graceful as a cat. Can't speak a word to them as they communicate by body movement and tonal changes in the flowerlike face. But at least they don't get in the way . . . and they are *great* traders!

More later. I'm going back down with the last shuttlecraft, to deliver the rest of the medical stuff. It's evening at the base there, and I want to see it in the light of the two moons.

Excerpt, Nipponese Influences in Federation Foreign Policies, by Pat N. Fredericks:

From the beginning there was a strong percentage of Starfleet personnel of Japanese descent. Far more than the Chinese, they took readily and quickly to the life in the stars. The Japanese, according to Cropsey, were always more adventurous, and their participation in the exploration of space, once the warp drive was introduced, was extensive.

Excerpt, My Voyage in the Enterprise, by Lieutenant Commander Lloyd Alden:

It was on the *Arcturus* that I first met the slender young helmsman of Japanese-Hawaiian descent who was to play such an important part in my life in the future. His name was Hikaru Sulu, a fairly new lieutenant with a couple of ships under his belt. We hit it off right away, and not just because we bunked together.

The *Arcturus* was the first heavy cruiser for the both of us. Since I'd been there several months, it was my turn to show him around. Those *Constitution*-class ships are big, and you could spend a lot of time just wandering around, but I took him to the rec room first. (This was the old-style rec room, the little ones they scattered all over instead of the bigger, central type they favored later on.)

First pop out of the tube in comes Lieutenant Naomi Rhada, an Asian lady, who brought out the old-fashioned cavalier in Sulu. Did everything they say not to do: pulled out her chair, got her a drink of Dilute (as we called it on those ships), and started going Warp 10 with the charm.

I'm not going to say any more, Naomi being the mother of three, married to a Marine sergeant-major, and a black belt herself. But we had some good times, despite what was pretty rigorous rules about the behavior of ship personnel and especially officers. But I knew this yeoman who . . . well . . . We served together a year, Sigma Mu IX to Rigel, over to some mudball at the edge of nowhere and back to Nu Xi XIII (I think they call it New Mars now). He got transferred to the *Enterprise* then, and I didn't get aboard until later.

Excerpt, At Warp Speed: Memoirs, by Lieutenant Commander Lex Nakashima:

Another of my friends aboard the *Enterprise* was Lieutenant Sulu. I guess at first it was just the racial thing, a couple of Orientals with all those Anglos, but I got to liking him, and we both had an interest in fencing.

Of course, fencing is absolutely vital a skill for a helmsman (him) and a laundry officer (me). We even got up a few classes, and darned if Captain Kirk didn't come around a few times and put on the mask and breastplate!

But we also shared an interest in exotic plants. I knew more about the Tellurian spit-gorm, but he was way ahead of me with the *Samekh*-9 and the Coridan creeper. He picked up a hoffman when we orbited Cleopatra-9, but Dr. McCoy saw it and marched Sulu and the creepy thing down to the transporter room and jettisoned it straight into a million cubic miles of nothing.

We also shared an interest in a yeoman named Rand but she had eyes only for the captain, so we forgot her and concentrated on a Sergeant Alicia Markova and a Loot named Karla Knutsson, from Vital Statistics and Library Facilities.

Excerpt, Interview with Lieutenant Naomi Rhada by UBC-TV reporter Mike Dell, dated 10 October 2167:

MD: How well do you know the other members of the ship's personnel?

NR: Depends what you mean by well. We all work very hard, and there is often danger. But we are not working every minute.

MD: How do you entertain yourself?

NR: I play chess a little. Once I even played Mr. Spock, though I was no competition. He plays the ship's computer all the time and usually gets a draw—which after all, is the best anyone can do, I imagine.

MD: What about more active pursuits?

NR: There is null-gravity ball, which is *very* active! You must work very hard. Do you know it?

MD: No, I've not been offplanet.

NR: Ah. Well, there is a spherical room, quite large. Only on the larger ships, of course. The artificial gravity is turned off. A line divides the sphere into two hemispheres, and there are circles and diamonds you cannot step into without losing points. You shove off, a ball is fired from the center line by computer, and you try to bat it into the opponent's goal disk. But without gravity you keep going until you hit something, so you must flip over to break your fall against the opposite spot, avoid a penalty zone, and be ready to launch again. Lieutenant Sulu is very, very good at this, very athletic, very supple. He's our champion, the Engineering champion, that is. The different sections play each other.

MD: This Sulu; what is he to you?

NR: A friend.

MD: Your smile says perhaps more than a friend.

NR: No, a friend. I met him first on the *Arcturus,* and he was very helpful to me. Nothing more. I have a fiancé back home in New Delhi.

MD: These voyages are long, five years and more. You have someone who will wait?

NR: Yes.

MD: Not many do. Do you plan to give up the Starfleet and marry him?

NR: He will wait. I think.

MD: You think. Meanwhile, there is this Lieutenant Sulu?

NR: He is very nice, yes. There are married officers in Starfleet who voyage together. Perhaps, if my fiancé does not wait . . .

Letter from Dawson Walking Bear to Martine Massoglia, his publisher, dated 8132.8:

In answer to your first question, I think the 1000-line screen edition is fine. I don't know what Sulu thinks yet, but he may go for it in reprint.

Your second question: We did the original paper when we were young officers. I was an ensign, he a lieutenant, and we were aboard the *Enterprise*. (Note: you might use that in publicity, the old ship being the glamour girl she is—and rightly so!)

The genesis of it was in 4598.0, when we hit Iotia. No one had been there for a hundred years, not since the old *Horizon* had stopped in pre-spacewarp days. The natives were humanoid but very, very imitative. Somebody left an old-style book there, one of those old things with pages and flat photos. It was called *Chicago Mobs of the Twenties,* about the criminals of the early twentieth century in North America. Darned if they didn't imitate everything, down to the clothes, old chemical-propellent weapons, and even the streets, though the buildings were false-fronted with the usual Iotian nestlike buildings behind, except for ceremonial rooms.

It was so intriguing that Sulu and I started writing the paper not long after: *Parallel Time Line Devel-*

opment was how we started, but over the month it moved into the paper you read, *Cultural Mockery*. Dr. McCoy (yes, *the* Dr. McCoy) read it and sent the text by subwarp to a friend of his from college who was in publishing. He rejected it, but Diane Russell, at Starwanderer Books, jumped on it.

We're glad you want to update it with additional cultural examples, which we can certainly do. If you can see your way to bringing it out with a flag to match my other books, I'd love it. Nothing like having reader identification when they are going through the menu on that old home screen and see something they remember.

Which reminds me, *Blood on the Moons of Omega IV* and *Killer Asteroid* are both coming up on release from Electrobook. They did well—partly due to the good photography by Emmett—and I'd appreciate it if you took a look and see if they might fit in, with a bit of rewrite, with your Space Adventurer series.

Will contact Sulu at first chance. He's on the *Enterprise*, of course, but I can put in a message with a package for high-speed blurt in subwarp whenever they check in with Headquarters again.

Excerpt, letter from Lieutenant John Kyle to Helen Kyle, undated:

Lieutenant Sulu has a pet. It's a semisentient Baldric plant which he thinks is female and calls Gertrude, but which Yeoman Rand says is male, and calls Beauregard. It looks like a long-necked pineapple, and I think it reminds Sulu of the Hawaiian Islands.

**Excerpt *(Declassified)* Service Record evaluation by Dr. Talal
Ben Abdullah, dated 3476.1:**

No doubt about it, subject is a confirmed romantic. Highly efficient, takes orders well and gives orders sensibly, and all the other good attributes of a field officer, but at heart subject is on a mission to find himself, to find "romance," and the sort of gallant action all romantics seek.

This is not to subject's detriment, as his record shows, but present and future commanders should be advised that there is no doubt subject sees himself as some kind of Robin Hood, Zorro, and perhaps Casanova, a flynn of the first order.

To put it in pragmatic terms: a man to have on your side, but trust him to perform the more romantic and gallant of any two actions.

Uhura, Nyota

SERIAL NUMBER: SP111-712

PRESENT RANK: Lieutenant Commander
BORN: Nairobi, United States of Africa, Terra, 24 October
    2140
FATHER: Damu Pua
MOTHER: M'Umbha Makia (deceased)
SIBLINGS:
    Malcolm Marien Uhura
    (Nyota Uhura)
    Uaekundu Uhura
MARITAL STATUS: Unmarried
CHILDREN: None
EDUCATION: Primary Nairobi; secondary Cairo;
    University of California at Irving, California, Terra;
    Starfleet Academy, Class 101
STARFLEET ACADEMY GRADE AVERAGE: 3.4
PRIMARY LANGUAGE: Swahili and English; also Universal
    English, Kikuku, French
COMMENDATIONS:
    Vega Award of Merit, Meteor Class
    Starfleet Unit Citation, with Two Clusters
    Starfleet Commendations: 18
AWARDS OF VALOR:
    Procyon Order of St. Mark
    Starfleet Citation for Exceptional Gallantry
    Federation Exceptional Service Medal
    United Federation of Planets Star of Valor
CONDEMNATIONS: None
STARFLEET ACADEMY DEMERITS: One
INTERESTS: Music; song writing; art; languages; African
    history; Arizal sculpture; running; Orion-dervived
    dancing; plays both Terran and Vulcan harp
STARFLEET ASSIGNMENTS:
    U.S.S. *Elst Weinstein*, NCC-6005 (Transport),
        Assistant Communications Officer
    U.S.S. *Azrael*, NCC-517 (Destroyer), Communications
        Officer

U.S.S. *Enterprise*, NCC-1701 (Heavy Cruiser), Chief
Communications Officer
Starfleet Academy, staff
U.S.S. *Hornet*, NCC-1714 (Heavy Cruiser), Chief
Communications Officer
U.S.S. *Enterprise*, NCC-1701 (Heavy Cruiser), Chief
Communications Officer
U.S.S. *Antares*, NCC-1820 (Heavy Cruiser), Chief
Communications Officer
U.S.S. *Enterprise*, NCC-1701 (Heavy Cruiser), Chief
Communications Officer

Excerpt, Romance in the Stars, by Diane Russell:

The Africa of young Nyota Uhura was not, in some
ways, much different from the Africa of her distant
ancestors. An hour's aircar flight from the gleaming,
air-conditioned towers of Nairobi, you could see a
herdsman tending his flock, hear the drums, smell
the dust and flowers.

The Africa of Tarzan, of Stanley and Livingstone,
of the two-dimensional motion pictures was still
there, although you had to search for it. In the great
animal preserves of Kenya time had not moved all
that much. True, the last remaining elephants were
tagged with transponders, their wanderings tracked
by satellite. The wardens patrolled in silent aircraft,
the visitors were closely watched, the poachers few
and ineffectual.

The real Africa of Uhura's childhood was in the
great pits of the mineral mines, the forest loggers,
the humming factories and power centers of Addis
Ababa, Nairobi, Salisbury, Johannesburg, Gambia,

and Kinshasa. But still, there were the festivals, the recreations, the cultural parks that preserved and relived the common ancestry. To hear drums while watching a holographic story about space travel was not uncommon.

The young Nyota—whose name means "Star" in the common trade language, Swahili—had feet in both worlds. Her roots were in the soil of an ancient land, but her heart was in the stars.

In *My Voyage in the Enterprise*, Lloyd Alden recalled a conversation with Lieutenant Uhura after a relaxing evening in the recreation room with friends. "She said, 'I used to love to go to Kenya, to the great park there. They had restored it to the way it was in the nineteenth century, with rough, dusty roads and villages. My first time there I went out at night—I must have been seven or eight—and I was just stunned! I had never seen so many stars. I had lived in Nairobi all my life, and like any great city, the lights block out the stars. The Milky Way, the lens of the Home Galaxy seen on edge, was the most spectacular sight I had ever seen! I knew then I had to go there.' "

In his autobiography, *Where No Man Has Gone Before*, James Kirk spoke of Uhura's early longing for the distant stars. "It was no secret that Uhura was a romantic. But that is hardly an uncommon condition aboard any starship. Romantics are basically restless, they want to see what is on the other side of the hill, the other side of a sun, the other side of the galaxy. It was just, perhaps, more obvious with Lieutenant Uhura."

In *Space, the Final Frontier*, Uhura's own account

of her years on the *Enterprise*, she wrote: "I went into the stars expecting. Expecting ... what? I had no idea. *Something*. Something different. Something new. I certainly achieved that goal. There were more 'somethings different' to be found than I could have possibly imagined."

Letter, Nyota Uhura to Maryanne Chungwa, a childhood friend, 19 March 2157:

I can't believe it! I received the notice from Starfleet Academy yesterday and I've been floating ever since! *I've been accepted!*

I know the work will be difficult. The drop-out rate is amazing, I've heard. The *failure* rate is even higher. But when you have gotten through the Academy, you have *done* something!

I guess I can tell you this now, but when you dropped out of good ol' Cairo U. to take an engineering post on that supply ship going to the moons of Jupiter, I *envied* you! Oh, I was so *jealous!* You were out there, seeing things for the first time, from *space*, and I was slugging it out at UC-Irvine and HAD NEVER EVEN BEEN OFF THIS MUDBALL OF A PLANET!

But now—aha!—*now* I'm going to Starfleet Academy. Look out, stars, here I come!

Letter, M'Umbha Malkia Uhura to Nyota Uhura, dated 12 June 2158:

My dear daughter:

Congratulations on completing your first year at the Academy! Your father, brother, and sister join me in wishing you well. We are sorry you cannot come home this summer, but we understand your desire to attend further classes in music, which you could not have time for during the regular semesters.

Your brother says that he must reluctantly report the death of Bruce, your favorite elephant, up in Kenya Park. Uaekundu says that she met a very nice young man while jetboating on Lake Victoria and that *his* brother is in your class at the Academy. Do you know a Fimbo Pua van Veer?

Father says the coffee crop is excellent this year and that we should do well on exports.

My love to you.

Excerpts, African Heritage, by Garrett Tubman Jacanarat:

. . . And our daughters, too, went into space. Uazuri Ngumi rose to the rank of Captain, commanding the *Laura Reinecke* in the Ceti-4 incident. Ingrid Tandiko was the Medical Officer aboard the transport ship *Bernard Zuber*, which brought the body of Richard Daystrom home to Earth. Mia Kinywa was the First Officer on the *Monitor* during the Schirmeister crisis.

But perhaps best known of all is Nyota Uhura, who served two distinguished tours of duty aboard the U.S.S. *Enterprise*.

. . . On the second tour, which began inauspiciously as a training exercise, the *Enterprise* was commanded by Captain Willard Decker, who was superceded by Admiral James Kirk. The story of their incredible journey into the heart of the fantastically vast complex that was "V'ger" has been told again and again, but it is to be noted that Lieutenant Commander Uhura served with distinction.

. . . And on completion of the task and the reprogramming of the V'ger complex, the *Enterprise* set off again on a limited tour of duty before Nyota Uhura was transferred temporarily to the *Hornet*.

Letter, Nyota Uhura to Maryanne Chungwa, circa October 2164:

I've met someone. Yes, that kind of "someone." He's handsome and strong, and so intelligent! When I say handsome I *don't* mean "pretty," like Henry Ngouabi. Handsome men are just as wrapped up in themselves as beautiful women so often are. Both are often shallow, as they have never had to stretch much—things were given to them, opportunities offered, events happened, lives disrupted simply because these beautiful creatures moved among us.

No, he's not pretty, but he certainly is handsome. A strong face, definite and clear, like he meant every feature. Nothing wishy-washy about him. Oh, his name, I forgot to give his name! Jomo Murambi. Isn't that a name? Shades of early twentieth century!

He's an officer in the Army of the United States of Africa, a captain no less. His unit is a special one, the Special Forces. He's Baker company commander and was wounded at Dar es Salaam in the riot there a year ago, the one started by the Tanzanian separatists.

I don't know where to start telling you about him.

Remember when we used to talk about our Perfect Man, how he could do this or that, be good at such-and-such and just as expert at something else? "Too perfect to ever exist." Isn't that what you said? Well, my childhood companion, you were wrong!

He has a good basso voice, loves to sing, plays the drums, the Terran *and* the Vegan guitars, has composed a few songs—but they were really marching songs for his company. He plays chess, is rated Computer Minus Three, which isn't bad, since Computer-Equal is as good as you get, really. He was a tree toppler in his teens, a roustabout in the Nudian Desert oil strike, and shipped out to the Martian Colony on a transport ship. But he got in trouble with a super there and they shipped him back. He's a black belt in traditional karate and would love to study null-gravity karate.

He reads! I mean *books*, not just 1000-line screen adventures. He has an original paperback edition of *The Butterfly Kid* and *Cops and Robbers*, hardcovers of *Cirque*, *Timescape*, and two Heinleins. He loves early science fiction, Louis L'Amour, Donald West-lake, Robert Parker, M'keel von Schroeder, Tasmeel the Andorian, and Kipling. The books have all been Pree-served, of course, Oh, and he likes old twentieth-century picture magazines!

He collects photos of nineteenth-century Africa and India, has the most beautiful greencat plant I've seen, and the most wonderful eyes.

I guess by now you are thinking, "Oh, over the edge—!" Well, you may be right. We went dancing last night at Hotel Casablanca, in that famous Sky of Stars room where they have the most beautiful projections on the dome, just like being in space, traveling through the stars. It seemed as though we were alone, although there were a lot of eyes on us. We danced and danced, and there was nothing to jar anything.

He was so handsome in his black uniform with the Special Forces tabs. I wore that gold dress you called "super-slinky," and we were a *pair*, let me tell you, Marryanne. Oops! A typo! Well, maybe that's Dr. Freud slipping through! Heaven knows he's the first man I've met who I'd even *consider* giving up space for. (Did I tell you I'm Communications Officer on the *Azrael* now? We're retrofitting the new phaser cannons in construction orbit, so we all have leave.)

There is one fact facing me that I just cannot dodge, however. *One* of us must give up his or her job. Either I stay planetside—or at best, take just months-long trip around the Solar System—or he does. The difficulty is, he has no desire to go into space, at least as a career.

It would not be the first time a woman gave up *her* career for her man. Maybe I'm just jumping ahead too fast! Maybe this is just a passing fancy for both of us. (Or one of us!) But he could not move easily into space. He'd be perfect as commander of security aboard some heavy cruiser, like the *Constellation* or the *Enterprise,* leading ashore the troops and all.

Yes, I know, we are not a military force, though we use military discipline. But it would be insane to go into unknown territory—*really* unknown territory— without the greatest variety of options possible. It would be like having only a stick of dynamite to kill a bug. You need all *sorts* of weapons, and the discretion to use or not use. A good sharp group of security personnel is just the right thing for planetfalls where you don't know what might happen.

But that means he'd have to go to Starfleet Academy or at least Security Forces Training Center, and that would be *after* he wanted to go into space. Even then there would be no real security that we'd be stationed aboard the same starship. Starfleet *does* try to accommodate married personnel, but you know bureaucracy.

So I don't know. But I think I'm in love, Maryanne, in love, really in love, for the first time.

I'm going back up to the *Azrael* tomorrow for a week's duty and I'll write more then. It will give me time to think. Meantime, Jomo has gone off to some little fracus at the border, but he has promised to bring me back something from Cairo.

Excerpt, INS report, dated 16 October 2164:

Dateline Obbia, Somalia Province, United States of Africa: Fighting broke out today in the troubled Somalia Province in East Africa when Tanzanian terrorists seized a supersonic jet with 312 aboard, including the Consulate General of the Arab Republic and Kenda Porter, the sultry star of *The New Thief of Bagdad* and *Queen of Sheba.*

The jet, grounded at Obbia International Airport, was successfully attacked by a crack unit of the U.S.A. Special Forces. All terrorists were killed, two passengers were slightly wounded, and the only Army casualty was its leader, Captain Jomo Murumbi, a veteran of nine years service.

Miss Porter pronounced the dead captain a "true hero" and said that she would make his life story her next holographic feature.

Letter, Nyota Uhura to Damu Pua, dated 5 March 2166:

Dear Father:

My next assignment is very exciting. I'm to be Chief Communications Officer aboard the *Enterprise!* It's a fine ship with a good record, and we will be beginning a five-year voyage not long after I arrive. I don't know now whether I will be able to get down to dirtside (as we say in Starfleet) or not. I hope so, but my connections are going to be tight.

I'm leaving the *Azrael* here at Pollox VI, taking a scout ship, the *Selinger*, to Upsilon Xi III. There I hope to catch a commercial liner (they tell me either the *Charles Lee Jackson II*, the *Falcon*, or the *Thrush*, depending; maybe even *Queen Elizabeth III*!) to Levitz-5. Then a short hop to Earth via Alpha Centauri! Is that not a 3-D map of Sector 9?

But to get aboard a cruiser going on a five-year—!

So just in case I can't get leave or arrive too late, I want you to know I love you all and hope you understand. This is the really big chance! Almost all of my other trips have been in and around space that was known, tamed, unsurprising. (Note that "almost." I'm so glad *some*, at least, were in uncharted territory.)

The new Starfleet policy of not sending survey ships into areas that have not been at least given a once-over by a heavy cruiser is probably a good one.

The big ships can handle a lot, take a lot, and, if they must, put out a lot.

So I'm really looking forward. My love, XXXXXX-XXXXXXXXXX!

Excerpt, Offworld, by Hikaru Sulu and B. J. O'Katwin:

We were on our way to Beta Aurigae when Uhura reported a distress call from Camus II. Captain Kirk took us there at once, but the landing party found only two left alive, Dr. Janice Lester and Dr. Arthur Coleman.

The surviving archeologists who had been exploring the ruins there were beamed aboard and told of the others dying of celebium radiation. What we did not know at the time was that Dr. Lester knew the secret of entity transfer.

It was to Uhura, in private, and later to others, that Dr. Lester revealed a grudge that had haunted her for years. Uhura told me, "She knew Captain Kirk when they were cadets at the Academy. She's very ambitious and they were once, briefly, in love. But her ambition was too raw for our captain, and he walked out on her. She never forgave him."

Uhura went on to say that Dr. Lester never realized that her own passions had forced the issue between them. "She spent years studying ship operations and thought a captaincy was her due," Uhura said. "She never understood that knowing *how* to pilot a starship is hardly the only factor in being a captain."

What happened next happened swiftly. Dr. Janice Lester effected an entity transfer, trapping Captain

Kirk in her body while she was in his. She effectively had taken over the *Enterprise*. She tried to kill her own former body with Kirk trapped within it, but was prevented by the return of the remainder of the landing party.

Dr. McCoy put "Janice" into sickbay, thinking that in some fashion she had gone insane, claiming to be Jim Kirk. Sedation effectively neutralized our *real* captain while the Lester/Kirk controlled the ship. The imposter decided to abandon "Janice Lester" at the Benecia Colony, thus getting rid of both her former body and the troublesome Kirk personality.

But the diversion of the ship made several of us suspicious. Commander Spock affected a mind meld with the imprisoned "Janice Lester" and found that, indeed, James Kirk's personality was within the female shell.

The Janice/Kirk became hysterical and tried Mr. Spock for mutiny. During the testimony both Dr. McCoy and Mr. Scott became convinced that an entity transfer had somehow been achieved and they were charged with mutiny. When Janice/Kirk called for a death sentence, we all knew that our real captain was not in command.

When we refused to obey the commands of the ursurper, the entity transfer began to weaken. Had Janice/Kirk been able to leave her former body behind, the retransfer could not have taken place and she would have been safe.

Dr. Coleman was appealed to by the now nearly hysterical Janice/Kirk, who agreed to "her" demands to kill everyone. But before that could happen the transfer broke, returning the real Janice to her own body and our captain to his body.

"She was insane with hatred," Uhura said. "She made a desperate, last, sad attempt to kill Captain Kirk, but collapsed in tears. Doctor Coleman was in love with her, and he promised to take care of her ever after.

"It was a very sad affair, but she had always thought the reason she had not been advanced to her own captaincy was that she was a woman. She never understood—in fact, she was probably incapable of understanding—that the real reason was that she had of very narrow understanding of other humans."

I remember Uhura sighing, then saying, "I can understand loving someone, and I can understand hating them when that love died. But I can't understand wanting to destroy someone you once loved."

Excerpt, The Tribble Manual, by Gerald Davis:

Tribbles come in a variety of colors: blond, beige, white, tan, and deep auburn, as well as a variety of soft pastel hues. They are small furry creatures that were introduced by a somewhat shady startrader named Cyrano Jones. He repeatedly refused to divulge the source of these almost featureless animals for fear of his monopoly being broken.

My theory is that they are a genetic construct of the facile scientists of the Romulan Empire, for while they seem warm and cuddly to human/humanoid races, they react adversely to the presence of Klingons, who are their genetic brothers.

Naturally, being liked by humans and humanoids, they would be carried to the far reaches of the human empire. They are highly prolific and are, in effect, born pregnant. (See "The Genetic Overlapping of Tribble Gestation," in *Science*, Vol. XXIV/C/23-5.)

The genetic engineering of the tribbles seems to be oriented toward complete compatibility with "anything that moves," as Dr. Leonard McCoy wrote, "Except Klingons, who refer to them as 'parasites.' "

The first encounter of human and tribble occurred aboard the U.S.S. *Enterprise*, Captain James T. Kirk commanding. The starship received an order from Starfleet Command to protect Space Station K-7, which had a load of valuable quadrotriticale grain in its storage bins and a gang of Klingons in its recreation rooms.

Under the terms of the Organian Peace Treaty, Klingons were allowed Rest & Recreation at this class of space station and at certain planetside bases of the M-3 class or higher. Their presence, however, made the manager of the station very nervous.

Captain Kirk was aware that the rare wheat was important, for it is a high-yield, perennial, four-lobed hybrid, the only kind that can grow and successfully survive on Sherman's Planet, a famine-struck Federation world near enough to the neutral zone to be in contention between the Federation and the Klingon Empire.

Involved as he was in an ongoing argument between a Federation Undersecretary for Agriculture, the Station manager, and his own distrust of the Klingons, Captain Kirk did not notice what was to develop as a far greater threat: the introduction of tribbles into human space.

Cyrano Jones had routinely docked at K-7 and had been much taken with the beauty and charm of the Chief Communications Officer, Lieutenant Uhura. "They seemed harmless enough," Nyota Uhura said later. "All they do is eat and, uh . . . multiply."

Dr. Leonard McCoy, Chief Medical Officer, said, "I discovered that they seemed to be born pregnant, an overlapping of functions which seemed astonishing and which I at first disbelieved. The more they ate, the more tribbles they had. Their amount grew logrithmically, not arithmetically."

James Kirk wrote, "They overpopulated the ship in no time from the single specimen brought aboard quite innocently by Lieutenant Uhura. There were tribbles all over the space station as well. Suddenly we were up to our communicators in soft, furry, cuddlesome tribbles! They especially loved the hybrid grain. I opened a storage bin and was inundated by tribbles—dead tribbles. It was then I discovered that the Klingons had poisoned the grain, hoping for a devastating famine on Sherman's Planet, and an emergency evacuation, to be followed by a swift Klingon takeover.

"When I discovered that Klingons do not like tribbles, and very much vice-versa, I was able to uncover a Klingon disguised as a Terran bureaucrat who had poisoned the grain.

"We forced the Klingons to back down, and my resourceful Chief Engineering Officer, Montgomery Scott, managed to beam aboard the remaining live tribbles, then lock tight our defensive screens. Our imaginations went wild as we thought of the Klingons extreme discomfort at the agitated trib-bles. Mr. Scott said that they would be 'no tribble at all.' "

Lieutenant Uhura was agitated herself to have to give up her delightful tribble, but knew it was for the common good. "If they weren't so marvelously fertile," she said, "they'd make the warmest of pets. But . . ."

Bibliography

ADMIRAL JAMES T. KIRK, Official Starfleet Record

ADRENALIN-BASED ANTIDOTE FOR HYPER-AGING RADIATION, AN, by Dr. Janet Wallace and Dr. Leonard McCoy

ADVANCED PHASER DESIGN, by E. D. Klein

AFRICAN HERITAGE, by Garrett Tubman Jacanarat

AKHARIN TO FLINT, by Lewis Singer and Ramona Aroeste

AMUSEMENT COMPUTERS OF THE LANGLEY CLASS, by John Meredith Matheson

ANDORIAN NERVOUS SYSTEMS, by Teresa Flynn, Sc.D

ANDROID DETECTION, by Wendy Allhuman

ANDROIDS, by Marc Daniel Mankewiewicz

ANTIMATTER, by Dr. Frances Evans

ANTIMATTER CONTROL, by Dr. Reuban Wincelberg

ARCHAEOLOGY AND ANTHROPOLOGY OFFICER TRAINING MANUAL, 7-45-A-14, Starfleet Printing Office

ARCHAEOLOGY UNDER DIFFERENT SUNS, by Galen Tripp, Ph.D

ANTHROPOLOGY ON PLANET M-113, by Robert and Nancy Crater

ARCHITECTURE OF NON-HUMAN SOCIETIES, by R. N. Harrison

ART OF THE EARLY SPACE EXPLORERS, THE, by Benjamin Camacho

ART OF THE STARS, by James Barr and George Bearcloud

ARTIFICIAL GRAVITY, by Carroll Carr

ARTIFICIAL INTELLIGENCE, by Forrest Daugherty

ASTRAL NAVIGATION, by Richard Daniels, Sc.D

ASTRAL NAVIGATION DURING WARP-DRIVE OPERATION, by Edward Bookman

ASTROARCHAEOLOGY, by Galen Tripp, Ph.D

ASTRU NECAS, by Nicholas Gheorghe Ceausescu

AT WARP SPEED: MEMOIRS, by Lieutenant Commander Lex Nakashima

BARBARIANS WITH SPACESHIPS, by John Gill

BATTLE OF CHERON, THE, by Sir Alfred Hume

BATTLE STATIONS!, by Ashley Gray, Weapons Tech, IV-Class

BEAUTIFUL MINOS, by the Minosean Chamber of Commerce

BERSERKER, by Vincent Sanderson

BIOSPHERE CONTAMINATION PREVENTION, by Richard Hammond

BLACK HOLES EXPLAINED, by Alder Danielson

BUILDING OF THE *ENTERPRISE*, THE, by Art Hagen

BURNT BY A HUNDRED SUNS; *The Story of Pavel Chekov*, by Beverly Beachwood

CAPTAIN CHRISTOPHER PIKE OF THE U.S.S. *ENTERPRISE*, by Roderic N. Berry

CAPTAIN WILLARD DECKER, by Neola Graef

CELLULAR METAMORPHOSIS: THE SECRET OF ANTOS IV, by Astrid Behr

CENTAUR IS JUST NEXT DOOR, by Mira Romaine, Commander, Starfleet

CHILDREN OF THE STARS: HUMAN EXPANSION 1990–2300, by Asenath Richards

CLOTHING & COSTUMES OF ALIEN RACES, by Kathy Miesel

CODE OF CONDUCT FOR STARFLEET SERVING OFFICERS, Starfleet Manual 1-99-0-325/1

COLLECTED TALES OF WARSPACE, edited by Joyce Martin

COLONEL PHILIP GREEN: THE BUTCHER, by Erwin Slavin

COMBAT WITH EDGED WEAPONS, by Paul Zimmerson

COMBATING ALIEN MIND-CONTROL TECHNIQUES, by Dr. Eric Pfeil, with an Introduction by Captain James T. Kirk

COMMON CODE OF JUSTICE FOR THE UNITED FEDERATION OF PLANETS, Edition 1/1a, United Federation of Planets Printing Office

COMPUTER TECHNOLOGY, by Weldon Associates

CONSTITUTION-CLASS STARSHIPS, by Hagen & Costa

CONTRACEPTION IN NON-HUMAN SPECIES, by Mirielle Hupp, M.D.

CORBOMITE MANEUVER: THE CLASSIC ALIEN ENCOUNTER, THE, by Tom Nellis

"CORDRAZINE: SOME ASPECTS OF OVERDOSE," by Dr. Leonard Mc-Coy, in *New England Journal of Medicine*

CORRECTIVE MEASURES, *An Account of Klingon Occupation*, by S. Dolinsky

COURT-MARTIAL PROCEEDINGS OF COMMANDER SPOCK, THE, Starfleet Records, declassified 8201.9

CREATIVE LIFEFORM, THE, by Canfield Grant

CREATIVITY IN NON-HUMAN LIFE FORMS, by Alicia Houston

CRISIS AT BABEL: THE FORMATION OF THE FEDERATION, by John Gill

CRYOSURGERY, by L. Clayton Johnson

CYBORGS, by Richard Hammond

DANCES OF ORION, THE, by Elizabeth A. Randall

DEATH OF CAPTAIN SPOCK, THE, by Randall Lofficier

DEATH OF THE *RELIANT*, THE, by Thomas O'Herilhy

DELTAN CELIBACY, by Neola Graef

DEVELOPMENT OF THE ROMULAN PHOTON TORPEDO, by Robert Tomlinson Martine

DIARY, by Janice Rand Dale

DICTIONARY OF MOONS, edited by Alana Frisbie

DILITHIUM CRYSTAL POWER GENERATION, Starfleet Manual 6-90-X-92

DILITHIUM CRYSTALS, by Commander Montgomery Scott, with Marc Bixbey

DISEASES OF SPACE, THE, by Dr. Roberta Armruster and Dr. R. N. Bounds

DRAGONS OF BERENGARIA VII, THE, by Sular, Chief of Exobiology, Vulcan Academy of Sciences

DUOTRONICS EXPLAINED, by Harris Daystrom, Ph.D

EARLY SPACE MEDICINE, by Dr. Joseph Boyce

EARTH THROUGH VULCAN EYES, by Tom Nellis

EINSTEIN TO DAYSTROM, by Raymond Capelli-12

EMINIAR VII DISRUPTOR WEAPONRY, by James Sperry Webbert

EMPATHS: NATURE'S MYSTERIOUS HEALERS, by Joanna McCoy, M.D.

ENCYCLOPEDIA OF ALIEN LIFE FORMS, 56th Edition, edited by Susan Lieberman

EROTICISM OF VULCANS, THE, by Maureen Lucas

EUGENICS WARS, by Kenneth Navato

EXOGEOLOGY, by Arthur Orinda-Widner

EXTRAGALACTIC CIVILIZATIONS, by Evanier Schneider

EXTRATERRESTRIAL LIFE, a memoir by Thomas Digby

EXTRATERRESTRIAL REPRODUCTION, by K. N. Rowland

FEDERATION WARRIOR RACES, by Andrew Bryne

FEINBERGER SERVICE AND REPAIR, by Caleb Paine

FIRST ENCOUNTER: *We Meet the Klingons*, by Sir Alfred Hume

FIRST WARP SHIP: THE STORY OF THE *BONAVENTURE*, THE, by George Leeper

FORMATION OF THE FEDERATION OF PLANETS, THE, by Dorothy Sandler

FREEDOM UNDER KLINGON RULE, by Anonymous

FROM DIFFERENT SEAS: EVOLUTION OF THE VULCAN RACE, by Dr. James Gregory and the Anthropology Department of Benford University

FROM THE *NAUTILUS* TO THE *ENTERPRISE*, by Thomas Scherman

FUNDAMENTAL DECLARATION OF THE MARTIAN COLONIES EXPLAINED, THE, by John Hammerlich, Former Governor of the Martian Colonies

FUSION PRINCIPLES, by Surak Benford

GENERAL ORDERS, Starfleet Command Directives

GENESIS PROJECT, THE, by Dr. Carol Marcus with Dr. David Marcus

GEOGRAPHICAL DICTIONARY OF FEDERATION PLANETS, Edited by Michael Fox

GEOMETRY OF WARPED SPACE, THE, by C. O. Leman-Sydney

GUIDE TO EXTRATERRESTRIAL LIFEFORMS, Second Edition, by Robert Null

HERITAGE OF CURIOSITY: THE HOMO SAPIENS INVASION OF SPACE, by Lynda Steffan And Daniel Arlington

HIS NAME IS MUDD: THE STORY OF HARCOURT FENTON MUDD, by Rebecca Patrick

HISTORY OF THE ROMULAN EMPIRE, by John Gill

HISTORY OF THE SAN FRANCISCO NAVY YARD, *From Shoreline to Starline*, by Penny Adams

HOSHI TABI SURU, by Reiko Izuno

"Improvised Power Generation," by Commander Montgomery Scott, excerpt, *Warp Drive Engineering News*, Vol. 832

IMPROVISED WEAPONRY, by E. D. Klein

IMPULSE ENGINE MECHANICS, by Richard Hammond

IN THE HIGHEST TRADITION, by Admiral Jay J. Mallory

INCIDENTS PERTAINING TO SAVING EARTH, by the Staff of *Universe*

INTELLIGENCE MAGNIFICATION, by Dr. Francis Franz

"Internal Federation Policies Regarding Free Planets," uncredited, excerpt, *Federation Diplomat Digest*, Vol. 399

INTERSTELLAR LAW, by Supreme Court Justice Henrietta Manning

KAHLESS THE UNMERCIFUL, by Asimov Coleman

KHAN NOONIAN SINGH: THE YEARS ON EARTH, by Gene Wilbur

KHAN NOONIAN SINGH: THE YEARS IN EXILE, by Gene Wilbur

KINGDOM OF MEDUSA, THE, by Maxwell Seki

KIRK, by José Domingues

KIRK, by Areel Shaw, with Lawrence Van Cott

KLINGON ART FORMS, by Karissa Enzenbacher

KLINGON BATTLE TACTICS, by Kalisher Pelz

KLINGON CUISINE, by Kalisher Pelz and Elaine Granada

KLINGON EMPIRE, THE, by Lisa Araminta

KLINGON INVOLVEMENTS: POLITICS IN SPACE, by Kelso Butner

KLINGON PSYCHOLOGY, by Kalisher Pelz

KLINGON REPRODUCTIVE CYCLES: SOME COMPARISON TO VULCAN PSY-
SIOLOGY, by Teresa Flynn

KLINGON TRADITIONS, by Suzanne Potter

KLINGON WEAPONRY, by James Sperry Webbert

KLINGON WEAPONRY AND TACTICS, by D. Arthur Grennell

KOLINAHR AND THE VULCAN WAY OF LIFE, by Lisa Araminta; Introduction by Larek

KZIN, THE, by Lawrence van Cott

KZIN COMBAT TECHNIQUES, by Fleet Admiral Gregory Calkins

KZIN WARRIOR TRADITION, THE, by Lawrence van Cott

LE MAIRE'S ASTROMAPS, *Edition CLIV to CCIX*

LIGHTNING IN THE MUD: *Evolution on Non-Human Species*, by
Franz Frank

"Magnetic Organisms," by Dr. Leonard McCoy, excerpt, *Rigellian Journal of Medicine*, Vol. 303

MAN CALLED FLINT: GENIUS OF TIME, THE, by Tom Nellis

MASTER COMPUTERS, by Steve Langley

MEDICAL ASPECTS OF PROLONGED EXPOSURE TO ALIEN SUNS, by Dr.
Alana Trimpi

MEDICAL EMERGENCIES IN HOSTILE ENVIRONMENTS, by Dr. Leonard
McCoy and Dr. Christine Chapel

MEMOIRS, by Dr. Leonard McCoy

MEMORIES OF DISTANT STARS, by Naomi Rhada, Lieutenant Commander

MEMORY ALPHA I: SUM KNOWLEDGE, by Jessica Wolfman

MEMORY ALPHA II: RENAISSANCE, by Jessica Wolfman

MENACE OF FEDERATION INVASION, THE, by General K'tar, Order of
the Klingon Star, translated by Bedar Turak

METRONS, THE, by Frederick Pevney

MID-RANK RIGHTS AND PRIVILEGES, by Marion Workman

MILKY WAY GALAXY, INHABITED PLANETS ROSTER, Edition 313,
United Federation of Planets

MIST/FIREFLIES/STARS/US, by Lawrence van Cott

MODERN WEAPONRY, by E. D. Klein

MÚZHESTO, by Vsevolod Skoropadsky, Simon Krushevsky, R. I. Khatisian

MY VOYAGE IN THE *ENTERPRISE*, by Lieutenant Commander Lloyd Alden

MY YEARS OFF EARTH, by Admiral Louis Gray

NIPPONESE INFLUENCES IN FEDERATION FOREIGN POLICIES, by Pat N. Fredericks

NON-HUMAN COMMUNICATIONS: GRUNTS TO TELEPATHY, by Arthur Marano

NON-HUMAN REPRODUCTION METHODS, by Dr. Kenneth Butterfield

NON-HUMAN WRITING: CLAY TO ELECTRONS, by Lydia Ventura

NULL-GRAVITY COMBAT, by Fleet Admiral Gregory Calkins

OFFWORLD, by Hiraku Sulu and B. J. O'Katwin

OFFWORLD COOKERY, by Elinor Francis

ONE SMALL STEP FOR A MAN, by the Staff of Canaveral Museum

ORION DANCING TECHNIQUES ADAPTED FOR HUMAN USE, by C. C. Chapman

ORION SLAVE DANCERS, *A Visual Record*, by Kathy Sanderson

PAUL PIPER, HIS MEDICINE AND HIS TIMES, by Wayne Fox

PHASER DEVELOPMENT, by D. Arthur Grennell

PHASER MARKSMANSHIP STANDARDS, by James Sperry Webbert

PIRATES OF ORION, THE, Lieutenant Commander Arex

PLANETFALL, by Peter Kirk

PLANETFALL UNDER HOSTILE CONDITIONS, by Fleet Admiral Gregory Calkins

PLANS AND INTENTIONS, by Klaar, Chief Tactician, Klingon High Command, translated by Bedar Turak

PRECISE STELLAR MEASUREMENT, by C. Curley and B. Balfour

PRIME DIRECTIVE: ITS MEANING TO THE HUMAN RACE, THE, Martin Gerber

PURGING COMPUTERS OF EXTERNAL CONTROL, by Caleb Paine

RECOGNIZING EROTIC RESPONSES IN NON-HUMANS, by Ursula Dunn

RICHARD DAYSTROM, by Patricia Cook Richards

ROMANCE IN THE STARS, by Diane Russell

ROMANCE OF SPACE, THE, by Kathleen Bromont

ROMULAN ART FORMS, by Karissa Enzenbacher

ROMULAN CLOAKING DEVICE, THE, by Stephen David

ROMULAN COMBAT TACTICS, by Richard Reno Penny

ROMULAN MATING TECHNIQUES, by Marjorie Ellerson

ROMULAN STARSHIP DESIGN, by the Staff of *Starships!*

ROMULAN WEAPONRY, by James Sperry Webbert

ROUTINE PATROLING, Starfleet Manual 1-22-R-56

RYETALYN AND RIGELLIAN FEVER, by Dr. Doreen Webbert

SAREK, THE GREATEST VULCAN, by Larek

SAREK AND THE HUMAN, by Lisa Araminta

SARGON: THE LAST OF HIS KIND, by Mervyn Stevens

SARPEID HISTORY, by John Gill

"The Saurian Virus," by Dr. Leonard McCoy, extract, *New England Journal of Medicine*

SCALOS: ACCELERATED LIFE, by John Warrington

SCOTTISH LAD GOES TO THE STARS, A, by Robert Braffyll Shaw

SCOTTY, THE STORY OF A STARMAN, by Lisa Araminta

SEXUAL TENSIONS ON INTERSTELLAR VOYAGES, by Victoria Komen, M.D.

SHAPE-CHANGERS, by Astrid Behr and Greg Anderson

SHIPBOARD ETIQUETTE, by Ronald Fair Wilson

SHORT HISTORY OF THE UNITED FEDERATION OF PLANETS, by Elizabeth Palmer

SLEEPER SHIPS OF THE LATE TWENTIETH CENTURY, by R. T. Hevelin

SPACE, THE FINAL FRONTIER, by Commander Nyota Uhura

SPACE ARMOR, by Gilman Christopher

SPACE LAW, by Samuel T. Cogley

SPOCK, THE HUMAN VULCAN, by Lisa Araminta

"Stardates Explained," by B. J. Turnbull, excerpt, *The Space Tourist's Handbook*, 2nd Edition

STARFLEET, by Commander Larek

STARFLEET ACADEMY, by Admiral Pim de Vries

STARFLEET ACADEMY RULES AND REGULATIONS, 17th Edition

STARFLEET CHRONOLOGY, Volumes 18–22 (Declassified)

STARFLEET COURTS MARTIAL PROCEEDINGS, Starfleet Manual 1-1-6a-B-23

STARFLEET YEOMANRY, Starfleet Manual 12-101-E-213

STARFLEET'S OTHER SHIPS, by Dian Ardmore Crain

STARSHIP CONSTRUCTION, by Joel Costa

STARSHIP CREWMEN UNDER STRESS, by Dr. David Marano

STARWARP: *The Autobiography of Edward Leslie, Commander, Retired*

STELLAR DIPLOMACY IN THE AGE OF CONFRONTATION, by Richard Hoberg

STELLAR ENGINEERING, by Russell D. Manning

STORY OF THE U.S.S. *EXETER*, by Morgan Tracey

STRATEGY AND TACTICS, by Admiral James T. Kirk

STUN PHASER RESPONSES IN HUMAN AND NON-HUMAN NERVOUS SYSTEMS, by Dr. Alan Walser and Dr. Alexis Trimpi

SURAK THE VULCAN, by Asimov Coleman

SUBSPACE COMMUNICATION, Starfleet Manual 3-892-C-23b

SUBSPACE RADIO PHYSICS, by Sir Andrew Commingore

SUPERNOVAS, by Abbé Gregor and the Science Department, Benford University

SURVEY SHIPS: THE FIRST TO KNOW, by Gene Fontana

TACTICS IN SPACE WAR, by General Sandra Cohen

TALES OF SPACE, by Robert Silverman

TALL SHIPS: *The Starships of Terra*, by Theodore White-Steffan

THE TALOS TABOO, by Sir Alfred Hume

TERRAN DOGS, by Kang, Captain, Klingon Star Fleet

THOLIAN FIEF, THE, by David Thorne-Kailua

THREE-DIMENSIONAL CHARTS OF FEDERATION BOUNDARIES, Starfleet Commercial Sales Division

TIME IN SPACE, by the Andruschak Space Laboratory

TIME TRAVEL, by Lawrence van Cott

TOTALITARIAN GOVERNMENT FORMATS: Three *Aspects of Societal Formation in Planetary Cultures*, by Harlan Steranko

TRANSPORTER PHYSICS, by Calvin Patten

TRANSPORTER TARGETING AND ACQUISITION, by Caleb Paine

TREATMENT OF XENOGRAPHIC DISEASES, by Kalea Edwards

TREK TO THE STARS, *The Story of Human Exploration*, by Christopher Lloyd

TRIBBLES ARE NO TROUBLE, by K. P. Malcor

TRIBBLE MANUAL, THE, by Gerald Davis

TRIBES OF CAPELLA IV, THE, by Teer Leonard James Akaar

UNDEFEATED: STORIES OF THE GREAT STARSHIPS, by Dian Ardmore Crain

UNIVERSAL TRANSLATOR SERVICE AND REPAIR, by Caleb Paine with Dorothy-2

UPGRADING STARSHIPS, *Techniques & Procedures, Amended*, Starfleet Manual 92-6a-G/4-1

UNIFORMS, STARFLEET, Starfleet Manual 162-5-U-8/2

USE AND MAINTENANCE OF BLOOD-ANALYZER UNITS, General Electromedical Corp., 4th Edition

USED STARSHIPS, *A Renovation Guide,* by Lotus Newman & Hulan Davidson

U.S.S. *ARCHON, THE,* by Brioni Haig

U.S.S. *ENTERPRISE* SHIP'S LOG (Declassified)

"U.S.S. Jon Trimbal: The Lost Starship Nobody Remembers," by Betty McCarthy, *Stardate Evening Post,* Vol. XXXIV-3-C2

VESSEL INTEGRITY AT SUBLIGHT VELOCITY, by Donald Ivy

VOYAGES OF THE *CONSTELLATION, THE,* by Neola Graef

VOYAGES OF THE *CONSTITUTION,* by Halea Graef

VOYAGES OF THE *CORIDAN QUEEN,* THE, by Captain Meg Barish

VOYAGES OF THE U.S.S. *ENTERPRISE: A Semiofficial Account,* by John Griffin

VOYAGES OF THE *FARRAGUT,* SHIP OF THE LINE, by Shelly Friedman

VOYAGES OF THE U.S.S. *HOOD,* by Marc Carabatsos

VOYAGES TO DISTANT STARS, by Prince Makhosini

"VULCAN ACADEMY OF SCIENCES," by Jean Sackett, *System Newsnet*

VULCAN CONCEPTS OF TIME AND SPACE, by Saalin

VULCAN: PLANET OF LOGIC, by Parkdale Van Hise

VULCAN PSYCHOLOGY, by Michael Simmons and Saarek

"Vulcan Seas," by Noel Haagen-Simpson, *Science,* Vol. XXXIV-7-C3

"Vulcan Was Visited by Ancient Astronauts," by Tracy Lodge, *Exposé Interplanetary,* Vol. XXX-5C-13

VULCANS HAVE NO MYTHS, THE, by Lisa Araminta and Neola Graef

VULCANS IN HUMAN SPACE, by Tom Nellis

WARLOCK WITH A WAND, *The Story of Korob and Sylvia,* by Anthony Schneider

WARP DRIVE ENGINES, by Yuan-Shih-chang and Casimir Sigismund

WARP ENGINE MECHANICS AND THEORY, by Zefrem Cochrane VI

WARP STRESSES IN REAL TIME, by Richard Hammond

WATCH OFFICER HANDBOOK, by Galvin Condra

WATER PLANETS, by Astrid Behr and Greg Anderson

WHAT TO DO WITH A PREGNANT TRIBBLE, by Gerald Friedman

WHERE NO MAN HAS GONE BEFORE: *The Autobiography of James T. Kirk*

WIN BY ANY MEANS, by Subcommander Tal, Grand Navy of the
  Romulan Empire

XENOAROSTIA, by Dr. S. G. Davis

XENOBIOLOGY, by Dr. Leonard McCoy

XENOBOTANY, by Dr. Ismail al-Ashari; Introduction by Hikaru
  Sulu

XENOGRAPHICS, by John Summitrose Lacky

XENOPHOBIA: *Its Cause and Cure Through Communication*, by
  Elizabeth J. McCarthy, Ph.D.

XENOPOLYCYTHEMIA, by J. Kinney Canfield, M.D.

ZIENITE MINING TECHNIQUES, by Kent Fuentes